THE ANCIENT FAE

THE WORLD OF FAE
BOOK 4

TERRY SPEAR

PUBLISHED BY:

Wilde Ink Publishing

The Ancient Fae

Copyright © 2010 by Terry Spear

Cover Copyright by Terry Spear

Discover more about Terry Spear at:

http://www.terryspear.com/

SYNOPSIS FOR THE ANCIENT FAE

Princess Ritasia misses the adventure of getting her brother and cousins out of trouble, but when the hawk fae king arrives to court her, she becomes involved in trouble nothing like she's ever faced before.

The hawk fae king, Tiernan, must find a bride, but being a tyrant king, or so his people believe, he must find a woman who would help him to change his people's view of how he and his queen shall rule.

Princess Ritasia isn't anything like what he'd envision his queen would be like. Rough and tumble, unafraid of danger, and speaking her mind, the lady might just be the one for him.

The princess believes the king is a tyrant, at least at times. But she discovers he's not all that he seems, and she wants to learn even more.

The problem is that Ritasia stumbles across an ancient queen's magical artifact and nothing will ever be the same between her people, his, and what is dug up at the ancient fae dig site.

1

_____

Overhearing her brother's raised voice in his bedchambers, Princess Ritasia could only guess who he was speaking to as she was making her way to her own bedchambers, intending to change clothes and take a jaunt somewhere, someplace forbidden. The corridor was cooler now with the advent of fall. The autumn wind whistled outside the ancient stone walls of the castle, filtering through every crack and crevice. The tapestries depicting fae on horseback hunting or fighting could not keep the cold from finding a way in.

She shivered in her pale blue gown and realized if she was going to stay in this part of the world, she needed to put something warmer on as the temperature had surely dropped even from the time she had risen this morning. Paused near her brother's door, she was not about to venture past it until she heard all that was said between her brother and cousin.

She _could_ walk on past so they could see she was here and could overhear them, allowing her brother to decide if he wanted her to witness the confrontation or not. But she wanted to know what was up as this affected her also. And she wasn't sure he would allow her to listen.

Since Deveron hadn't shut his door, how did he expect to have a private conversation anyway? The fault was not her own that she overheard them.

"Micala, you will not see Cassie any further. And *that* is my final word on it," Deveron said, his words harsh.

"She is waiting for me at the ice cream parlor in South Padre Island, as we speak, my lord. I have to at least go there and tell her something." Micala wasn't backing down, which wasn't really like him when faced with her brother's wrath and didn't bode well, though Micala couched his own hot temper with an attempt to make an appeal to the crown prince of the dark fae.

"I will not permit it. You were only to pay attention to the human girl a couple of times under my direct orders, not to make such a big deal of this," her brother snapped. "If my mother learns of your continued association with Cassie, your proverbial goose will be cooked. It does not matter that you're her favorite nephew. She will not permit it. Do I make myself perfectly clear on this issue?"

Micala didn't say anything in response. Ritasia barely breathed, hoping her cousin would agree with Deveron before it was too late. Deveron was right. Micala had no business seeing the human girl beyond what her brother had expected of him in the first place.

And with Micala's continued persistence in seeing Cassie, the rift between her girlfriend Alicia, who was Deveron's betrothed, and Deveron, was ever widening. Which really infuriated Deveron.

"I have to see her," Micala said, as if the prince had not just made a ruling.

Deveron's command was always final. Just as when their mother, Queen Irenis, dictated to her courtiers. The only one who could change his ruling was the queen herself. Micala knew that. Why was he being so obstinate about it?

Micala continued, "We were to meet at the ice cream parlor in South Padre Island. Let me see her and call things off between us."

"You should have done so long before this. I have warned you in the past. If you do not agree with my rule, I will call the guards," Deveron threatened, his voice low, dark, and perfectly even. She knew when he took that tone of voice, he was on the verge of throwing their cousin in the dungeon of the Denkar castle, manacled against fae travel until Micala did what was right. Though she knew Deveron only thought to protect him, to keep their cousin safe should their mother learn Micala was still seeing the human girl and growing too fond of her.

Ritasia liked Cassie, who was spirited and friendly, and she had no wish for her feelings to be hurt. But they were bound to be, one way or another.

"If you do not see her, she will be upset, Micala. But she will have to learn that you are *not* coming back and move on. She will find someone else. Someone human. As it should be." Deveron was again the voice of reason.

Micala didn't respond.

"*Don't* make me force you to mind me," Deveron said, growling low.

"I will stay," Micala said, sounding highly frustrated. "If it pleases your lordship, may I leave?"

"By your own word, you will not meet up with her, Micala." Deveron waited for his cousin to agree.

After a long pause, Micala finally said, "Aye."

He sounded defeated, but Ritasia would try to smooth things out with Cassie and let her down as gently as she could while helping Micala out at the same time. She returned to her chambers to change clothes so she could be dressed appropriately for the human world. Now that she had a real mission in mind.

She pulled out one of her drawers filled with human clothes and slipped out a shimmering blue bikini. South Padre Island was still warm this time of year. And then she grabbed a flowery silky sheer skirt sarong and a pair of golden sandals. Quickly, she changed out of her gown and dressed for the warm island temperatures.

She would see Cassie, tell her something—she wasn't sure what yet—and then Ritasia would have fun with a guy—beach-time cute. Only he had to be without a girlfriend. Many of her female kind wouldn't care if a guy was alone or not. They'd just butt in and stir up trouble between the happy human couple. If the guy was too fickle to stick it out with his girlfriend and threw her over for a fae, he deserved what he got.

At least that was most fae's feelings on the matter.

But Ritasia wasn't interested in getting a guy like that to take notice of her.

Though she was supposed to always have an escort with her, she had never allowed that rule to stop her before. Without a word to anyone, she transported herself to South Padre Island, planning to visit her favorite ice cream shop, locate Cassie, and commiserate with her about how unfaithful men were, then take off down the beach to look for a nice fun human guy to spend the afternoon with.

The warm salty air swirled about her, catching her silky scarf skirt and tugging at it, when she noticed the wall that had been illustrated with graffiti, compliments of the winged fae. It appeared that humans had finally managed to cover her cryptic fae message with several layers of white paint. At least she assumed they had. Maybe her own people had done it.

She turned to head for the ice cream parlor where she'd get a nice hot fudge sundae while she tried to make Cassie feel better. But as soon as she turned around, she nearly ran straight into an unseelie fae, who was invisible to humans. Why had the blasted unseelie not even attempted to avoid running into Ritasia? The unseelie had seen Ritasia first and could easily have moved out of her path! In fact, she should have gone far out of her way to avoid any confrontation.

Ritasia glowered at the fae. The unseelie's red hair was piled on top of her head with silver combs, her skin white, eyes ringed with silver, unlike those of the seelie whose eyes were ringed with gold when angered. Which meant the unseelie was in a highly irritated mood already. She was wearing a teeny weeny bikini of white that was barely big enough to cover all the parts that needed covering.

Although Ritasia was wearing a bikini also, as she planned to catch a guy's eye after she saw Cassie, and when she found the right target, her bathing suit wasn't half as skimpy as the one the unseelie was wearing.

The girl, not much older than Ritasia, gave her a harsh look in return as if daring her to do something about her behavior, then continued on her way. Ritasia glanced back to watch the unseelie, who were said to have once been part of the seelie court. But one faction split off from another and waged war for so long against the other, using magical weapons of mass destruction so that another queen could rule in ancient times, the fabric of the world had been ripped in two, creating two separate fae planes. And then of course there was the human plane where both unseelie and seelie could visit. But they normally avoided confrontation when they ran across each other in the human world.

Like the seelie, the unseelie could be good, and they could be evil. So just being an unseelie didn't equate to all bad.

Ritasia watched as a young blonde, blue-eyed boy, studied the flight of a Monarch butterfly in his path, fascinated, chubby cheeks dimpled, mouth lifted as he walked beside his mother. And then the unseelie drew near him, and Ritasia knew she meant to do something bad. Kill the butterfly? Or something else?

Something else. She stuck her foot out and tripped him. He landed on his bare knees, bloodying them on the rough concrete sidewalk, and he started bawling.

Ritasia wished she could have thwarted the unseelie, although she knew it wasn't something she should have interfered with anyway.

The unseelie had moved past the boy but looked over her shoulder to gloat at what she'd done, as if the deed had given her a bit of evil pleasure. Then she saw Ritasia casting her a devil of a glower. The unseelie offered her a simpering smile and blew her a kiss as if to say, *Love the humans if you wish, but they're in my way.*

Not that Ritasia didn't feel similarly when humans got in her way, but clearly the boy had *not* been in the fae's path. The unseelie could very well have stayed out of his way.

The boy's mother lifted him into her arms and cooed to him, and his cries quieted.

Not all unseelie were bad, Ritasia reminded herself. And it was none of her business as to what the unseelie was up to.

She turned around to walk to the ice cream parlor and saw a cute guy stalking up the sidewalk in her direction, tanned, tall, and dark chocolate eyes that caught her gaze, and he smiled. Now *he* was just what she had in mind. He could even buy her the hot fudge sundae, and then she'd see Cassie and tell her...well, she still wasn't sure what to tell her that wouldn't hurt her feelings too badly. But Micala couldn't see her any longer.

Suddenly the human guy waved in Ritasia's direction, and she looked back to see who he was waving at, figuring she'd already lost her prime catch for the day.

Then she saw who it was. Who else but that blasted unseelie in the too-small bikini! And now *she* was heading straight for him, a thin smile stretched across her face, her green eyes sparkling with the devil. She was now very much visible in that scrap of a bikini, waving at him as she hurried to join him.

He looked over his shoulder as if he wasn't sure she really meant him, but then she said in a sickly-sweet tone that didn't suit the witch, "Tom, is that you?"

He cleared his throat, his cheeks and neck tinged with color. "Uh, no, I'm Mike. I guess you thought I was someone else."

Ritasia wanted to laugh at the unseelie's attempt to woo him. He looked a little disappointed. Here he thought some really hot chick was interested in him.

The guy focused on the unseelie's barely-there bikini and more importantly, all her naked skin, when Ritasia made her move. Though she knew better. But the unseelie really irked her.

"Mike," Ritasia said, smiling brightly, walking toward him, too. Her bikini wasn't as risqué as the unseelie's, but Mike's tongue was hanging out just the same as his gaze shifted over her figure, then caught hold of her gaze and held it.

Yeah, he was interested in her. Maybe her dark hair and eyes appealed more than the redhead's coloration. Or maybe he thought the redhead's bikini was a little *too* revealing, and he wanted a girl who wasn't such a show off. Or maybe he liked that she had called him by his real name.

He might have thought it was his lucky day. But when a seelie and an unseelie wanted to play with the same human, he was deadly mistaken.

Ritasia *knew* better than to make a move on him. She had been trained to avoid the unseelie as they seemed to have been taught to leave the seelie alone. But Ritasia couldn't help herself.

The unseelie *wasn't* about to let her prey go either though. "Mike, of course, from..." Ritasia hesitated, letting him tell her just where he was from.

"I'm a local," he said.

Wow, great tan, great body, *great* smile, Ritasia thought.

"I come here all the time," Ritasia said, which she did, when she could. "You could say I'm *almost* a local."

"Cool," he said, looking unsure as to who he should make the play for. It should have been obvious, Ritasia thought.

Then she smiled brightly. "When I was here last, you said you would take me for a hot fudge sundae."

The guy cast another 1,000-watt smile and said, "Sure," knowing he hadn't, but he seemed totally willing to play the fae's game. Humans always were. Hot guy, cute willing chick. Easy prey for a female fae.

The unseelie looked as though her wind-tossed hair could become writhing red coral snakes, and she would turn Ritasia into stone if she glanced in her direction again.

"Ritasia!" a male fae shouted.

Crap! Her brother, Deveron, his voice highly agitated, with an undercurrent of concern.

Ritasia swung around, her whole body heating. Deveron was dressed in jeans and a T-shirt and sneakers. He probably had gotten word about her being here unchaperoned and had thrown on some human clothes to intercept her. Unless...unless he was checking on Cassie and making sure that Micala hadn't popped over to see her despite Deveron's ruling. Maybe *he* was planning on telling her Micala couldn't see her any longer.

Deveron glanced at the unseelie, gave her a dark look, and spared the human an even hotter look as if to wordlessly tell him to leave before he really got himself into a pit of venomous snakes.

Then Deveron reached Ritasia. "We had a date, remember?" He sounded like a miffed boyfriend.

Her skin heating, she clamped her lips tight. Then she smiled, figuring a way to solve the issue of who Deveron was and said, "Mike, I'll have to take a rain check. My brother needs me." She knew her brother would not permit her to stay. Not right now, anyway.

"Brother, my butt, *Ritasia*," the unseelie said, sneering.

"Princess to you, jealous fae," Ritasia retorted, before she could watch what she said.

The girl's brows arched. "Princess of some fantasy world in your mind?"

Ritasia glanced at the guy, realizing he was waiting for her to explain what she meant.

She couldn't.

"Come on, Mike. You can get me that sundae instead." The unseelie took his hand and pulled him toward the ice cream parlor, but he glanced back at Ritasia, and she knew he had wanted to be with her, not with the redheaded unseelie. Or maybe he was still puzzled about her saying how she was a princess and the other was a fae, and he wondered where she truly was from.

When they had disappeared inside, Deveron grabbed Ritasia's arm. "What is the meaning of you telling that human you are a princess and the unseelie was a jealous fae? I leave you alone for one minute, and the next thing I know you're trying to start a war with the unseelie?"

"One minute?" Ritasia shrieked. "You have not been around for days until you showed up this afternoon. And finally I see..." Well, she hadn't really seen him. Only overheard him dictating to Micala. She jerked her arm free and folded her arms across her chest. "How did you know I was here?"

Deveron snorted. "One of our fae saw you and reported just the trouble you were about to get yourself into."

She wondered if Deveron had sent someone else then, to ensure Micala didn't try to meet with Cassie. Only instead he saw Ritasia mixing it up with an unseelie and returned to the castle to warn Deveron right away. "Which one was spying on me?"

Deveron smiled as if amused that she could not get away with anything. "I cannot say." Then he frowned. "Mother will have to find you work if you haven't anything better to do than start a battle with an unseelie."

"*Don't* tell Mother."

But the look on Deveron's face told Ritasia he might do just that.

Her safety was always tantamount to him, which despite being annoying sometimes, she had to love him for his concern.

"Besides, another lord has arrived to court you," he said.

She groaned. "I will only say no."

He grabbed her arm again, and right before he transported them, he said, "I know. I don't like *this* one at all, so you have my blessing and my support."

"Wait!" But she couldn't tell him she'd eavesdropped on his conversation with Micala and planned to see Cassie to tell her... something.

Deveron didn't wait, but returned her to the castle, to the great hall instead of her chambers, where she scowled at her brother as the lord who had come to see her stared at her open-mouthed, eyeing her bikini and grinned.

KING TIERNAN SCOWLED at the mess his father had gotten him into... all because the heartless man had to die.

Hawk fae kings were to immediately marry as soon as they were seated on the throne and a suitable bride could be found. Tiernan was supposed to consider the ladies his advisor believed would be suitable for matrimony, but he was tired of this whole kingship business. As soon as his father had died a week ago—the reason for his death still a mystery, but it was assumed by all he'd been murdered—Tiernan had had to take over the hawk fae kingdom at once.

He preferred hunting and fishing and fighting with his island neighbor, the griffin fae.

He still couldn't believe that he'd been recalled from exile—his father and he never having gotten along the few times he'd had to make courtly appearances, as if to ensure the prince was still alive and owed allegiance to the king—to be thrust into this position of power so all of a sudden. He'd expected his father to have lived for another hundred years or even centuries more. Wasn't that what always happened when tyrants ruled?

At least in the hawk fae kingdom it was known to be true. All the way back to his great-great-great-great grandfather, with a few more greats added to that, they had always been tyrants.

In almost every case, son had killed father, tired of waiting to rule from the seat of power. Which was one reason his father had exiled him. The whole situation was an irony. The king had to produce an heir to take over the throne upon his demise, but was afraid the son—or in some rare instances, a daughter—would shorten his rule should he or she be given the chance.

Legend had it that the queen always met an early death— ordered by the king himself, although it was said that a secret order of assassins was given the task. Why? Because two sons or a son and daughter could fight over ruling the kingdom. Civil war could ensue. So best to ensure the queen only had one offspring. And then, she no longer was needed.

He didn't know this for a fact as he'd never lived in the kingdom proper, but he was afraid the legends might be true. He knew only that his own mother had died at his birth, and he'd been raised by nannies in his own kingdom some miles away.

Despite that Tiernan *hadn't* been living within his father's castle walls, everyone in the kingdom knew beyond a doubt that he had murdered his father, like his father before him had done to his father, and so forth.

He didn't bother to correct their logic as they had in mind that it was true, no matter what he might say. It *was* tradition.

His people also seemed to fear Tiernan, as they did wisely of any of the hawk fae kings who had preceded him, which was also their custom. Which irritated him. He didn't like it that his people cowed their heads, wouldn't look him in the eye, and appeared to tremble when he drew near.

The thing with tradition and following the ancient ways was that breaking from convention made his people uncomfortable. They were used to everything being the way it was. And although he had no desire to be a tyrant and would not pretend to be, he knew his people still believed him to be. After all, he was his father's son, in a very long line of tyrannical rulers.

He sighed.

So now it was to be expected that the loveliest maidens from his kingdom and the minor kingdoms that bordered his region would be shown off to him as prospective brides, and he would choose one of them. And he didn't like the idea one bit. Not that he didn't want a wife. But he wasn't really ready for this. What if he chose the wrong woman? He wouldn't carry on the tradition of eliminating his wife after she had his child. Nor had he planned to banish his child from the castle after his or her birth. So he had to ensure he had the right wife.

Blond, blue-eyed Sophia, his most powerful mage, stood nearby smiling at him, as if he she was amused that he would be so annoyed over this whole affair. She seemed to be the only woman in the castle who not only was unafraid of him, but fluttered her eyelashes at him as if trying to get his attention.

Flirting didn't suit her. And beyond that, he wasn't interested. She was a mage. And though she was to be loyal to his rule, and his father's before that, he didn't entirely trust a woman who had such power, without even being a queen of the realm. If he made her his queen, she could wield even more power.

Romero, his human page, also stood nearby, a frown on his face. The perpetual 14-year old, though over a couple of centuries old— courtesy of the fae who had brought him to the fae realm and then died—was frowning at Tiernan. Romero could read anyone's mind, since none knew to shield their thoughts from anyone. No one else had such a gift and no one knew he had it either, except for Tiernan. Having become friends when Tiernan was exiled to the minor castle of the hawk fae along with Romero, Tiernan had brought him to the main castle as soon as he was recalled. Now he wondered why Romero was frowning. Had he read something in someone's thoughts that might cause difficulties for Tiernan?

Romero's face brightened a bit, and he caught the king's gaze and shook his head.

No matter how many years the king had known Romero, he could never get used to his reading his own mind.

For days, Tiernan had listened to his advisor present each beautiful woman in a long line of beautiful women, hearing all about their pedigrees and bride prices their fathers were willing to pay for the chance that their daughters would become queen and a son of hers would be king, someday. Tiernan wished to put off the selection. The problem was every woman looked at him as though he was a despot. Beyond that, most likely each woman suspected she would not live long after she had given him a child.

He sighed again. He needed to leave his kingdom far behind, and though his kind never ventured beyond the minor kingdoms of this hemisphere, except to fight with the major island fae kingdom nearby, he would leave and search for a maiden who would see him as who he truly was.

When a blue-eyed, dark-haired girl stood before him, eyes shimmering with tears, Tiernan turned to his advisor and said, "Enough, Lord Srenton!"

His advisor's jaw dropped, his gray eyes searching Tiernan's face as if he knew he was about to lose his position for failing to find the loveliest wenches in the realm and surrounding region that would appeal to the king. Maybe even his life.

"My lord—"

"Lord Srenton, either tell me our island neighbor is preparing war against us again and I must fight them, or I must journey to a place where our kind have never been."

Or at least for the most part. He was certain others had

ventured into other fae realms, but interaction with the other kingdoms that far away hadn't been a regular occurrence. He believed a
hundred and fifty years ago, a cartographer had mapped the
regions. And fifty years before that, a historian had made some
notes about the major kingdoms on the other side of the world. He
recalled some talk of the dragon fae and the lion fae having been at
odds with one another for centuries. He was glad in his hemisphere, the hawk kingdom was the only major realm on their conti-
nent. The only way the power would shift would be if some of the
minor kingdoms in the area united to fight the hawk fae. But
because of the ruling hawk fae kings' power over a millennium,
none of the minor kingdoms seemed to wish to challenge them.

Which was just as well.

"The griffin fae of the island kingdom do not appear to be
considering war at the moment, my lord. You are going to find a
maid from one of the other major kingdoms, I take it?"

"Mayhap."

Lord Srenton cleared his throat and looked gravely at him.
"Which major kingdom do you wish to see?"

"Any of them. All of them. Except for the island kingdom."
Tiernan shrugged. "Who knows where I might find the one
for me?"

"But the other major kingdoms are very warlike."

"Even the women?" Tiernan asked, surprised.

"Well, yes, my lord. Some of the women are better fighters than
the men, I've heard tell."

"I wish to see these warrior women." He smiled to himself.
Maybe a woman such as that would be able to handle being
married to a tyrant of a king and outlive him on the throne, even
after giving him a child.

Having heard the conversation between the king's advisor and
himself, Sophia said, "It is not wise to leave so soon after you have
just begun your rule."

Romero smiled, and Tiernan got the impression he agreed with the king, especially since he did not like the mage as she often belittled him because he was a human. He wisely did not voice his opinion though.

"When do we leave?" Lord Srenton asked, already knowing Tiernan well enough in the brief time they'd worked together that the king would not be stopped when he had something in mind to do.

But would his quest be fruitful, or would he have to return empty-handed and start all over again for a bride search closer to home?

2

A week after her near fight with the unseelie in South Padre Island and stalking out of the great hall in her bikini, after having said no to one more marriage proposal to a fae lord, Ritasia was finally allowed some freedom again. Her mother had taken away her ability to fae travel, punishment for not ignoring the unseelie fae like she should have done in the first place, but now she had it back. Yet, she knew her mother was planning something.

Ritasia didn't have a clue as to what it could be. But she knew from the sidelong glances her mother gave her, she was trying to figure out a way to ensure Ritasia didn't get herself into any further trouble.

The problem was Deveron had left her alone again. She was glad for her brother's interest in the dragon fae Princess Alicia, but she really did feel a bit...*lost.* She'd been so used to getting Deveron out of trouble, or covering for him, or even partaking in his mischievousness. But now that he was busy attempting to see Alicia on a daily basis, when he was ordered not to, Ritasia floundered as to what to do with her own time. She hated to admit it, but she was lonely.

She thought to involve herself in something adventurous, thrilling, dangerous, anything to chase away the doldrums. But what was there to do? She realized then that nearly every adventure she had taken part in had revolved around her brother or cousins.

She was forbidden to go to South Padre Island for another month, just in case the unseelie was still there, hanging around, maybe with reinforcements, just waiting to "play" with Ritasia some more in her dark way. And she'd never had a chance to see Cassie and tell her whatever she would have told her once she'd come up with something. She wasn't sure if Micala was staying away from Cassie or not, but she hadn't seen much of him either.

She opened her tower window as the seasonally cool breeze on the fall day swirled around her, smelling of crisp clean air. She considered the forest leaves flittering on the trees beyond the castle curtain wall in all their glorious colors—from purple to brilliant orange and bright red to sunny yellows while the grass and evergreens were still emerald green.

If she had even one artist's bone in her body, she would paint the scene and capture it for all time. Or at least until she could enjoy the fall colors next year.

Not that that would be adventuresome or dangerous. She sighed and rested her arms against the stone windowsill of the ancient castle, wondering whether she should take a jaunt to the human world today to some place that was forbidden.

At least forbidden to her if she chose to go alone. No place was truly forbidden to the fae. Except if she was the wrong sort of fae when she visited a location where another had called the territory their own.

But even Deveron almost always took a companion or two with him on his jaunts to the human world. She couldn't even bother with her cousin Niall, who was with the winged fairy, and Micala, who was getting himself deeper into trouble with the human girl Cassie, she was certain, despite Deveron's warnings.

Ritasia wasn't interested in any male she'd had to consider. Her mother had paraded a host of suitors before her all month long, attempting to get Ritasia's consent, yet she hadn't like any of the men. Either they were too old, or dull, or way too reckless. A couple even had human girlfriends, and she would not abide that.

She turned her thoughts back to where she would go and what she would do.

Before she could decide, which was another thing that was driving her insane—the inability to come up with exciting excursions that she could enjoy at the blink of an eye—a maid knocked at her chamber door and called out, "Princess Ritasia, Queen Irenis summons you to her solar."

That was not good. If only Ritasia had made a choice and already fae traveled, she would have been away and safe. When her mother summoned her for an audience, it was *always* bad news.

But then again, who would know if Ritasia had only *just* left the castle? Or had been gone before she received the summons?

And then she was decided. Ritasia transported herself in the fae way to the Dallas airport. She'd never been anywhere else in the human world but Texas. Time to see what else there was to explore.

She didn't even pay any attention to the flight she was getting on and didn't care, as long as she got away for the day. She didn't need a ticket or ID because she was invisible to the passengers.

Except for one.

Her back stiffened as she saw the male fae, his shimmering aura telling her he was invisible also, as his brown eyes darkened at spying her, and his mouth curved up a bit. He was tall and lean like her brother, with broad shoulders and a nice enough face. But he could be the most evil of fae. No one could tell by just a look.

When he quickly changed direction and headed straight for the plane she was taking, she felt her heart take off. She didn't have to bother with a passport or tickets so she stalked down the walkway to the plane.

When she was out of sight of the fae, she thought to transport straight back home. She didn't need a stalker fae on her trail. He wasn't one of her people, so he couldn't be tracking her, intending to return her to the castle. But she didn't know what he had in mind where she was concerned.

But why should she have to give up her quest for adventure because this guy was about to ruin it for her?

He was still trying to maneuver through the people standing in his way, which meant he was a pretty considerate fae to not walk straight through the passengers. He couldn't see her at this point, so she transported to another location in the airport.

But *she* walked through several people who were in her way. It didn't hurt them, as far as she knew. Just made them feel like body parts were falling asleep. But she wasn't going around them when she was in a hurry. Besides, she was a princess, and of the fae, and *they* should have moved out of *her* way. Not that they could see her. Or that they would know what she was if she revealed herself. But as much of a hurry as everyone was in, she didn't figure they would have moved aside to let her pass even if they did see her.

She hurried for another plane and intended to get on it before they'd even made first boarding call, although several passengers were already lined up and ready to board. Of course she would take first-class accommodation. If anyone sat in her seat, she would just move to one that wasn't occupied.

She instinctively glanced back to see if the man had followed her, but didn't see any sign of him, smiled, and headed down the walkway, wondering again what her destination was, but it was too late to check on it now.

She was seated in one of the more luxurious first-class customer seats when a white-haired man in a business suit tried to enter her row and sit on her lap. She considered letting him and making him numb until she moved, but then she sighed and moved over a seat. A white-haired woman joined him, and Ritasia scowled, walked through the people waiting to go to the second-class rows and sat in the window seat on the left side of the plane.

And saw the fae.

He was looking down at the floor of the plane, not in her direction. Then he looked at the seat where she'd first sat. He was tracking her fae dust. His gaze shifted to the seat where she was now sitting, and he smiled.

She shook her head at him and motioned for him to sit somewhere else.

He only smiled again and sat down beside her. She scowled, turned away from him, and peered out the window, hoping he would just vanish.

Instead, he leaned over and whispered to her, "Are you running away?"

She jerked her head around. "No! I'm..." Ritasia hesitated, then added in a hushed voice to the fae, "I'm taking a trip."

"You were going to Florida before. Now you're going to Scotland. Had you no preference for the place you would visit today?"

"Scotland?" she said, her voice raspy with surprise. She thought to go somewhere else in the States. Certainly not across the ocean.

"Which kingdom are you from?"

"Which are you from?"

"The hawk."

She stared at the fae with incredulity. "I've...never seen one of your kind."

He smiled again. She didn't care for his smile. It was more calculating than pleasant.

"And you are with which one?"

She had no reason to hide which fae kingdom she was with. They'd never had any trouble with the hawk fae on the other side of the world. "The lion fae."

Now it was his turn to look at her in surprise. "I have heard their women are warriors."

She lifted a brow.

He chuckled. "Mayhap we were misinformed."

"So who are you?"

"Brandolin, war minister to King Tiernan."

"You are here, looking to do battle with one of the kingdoms?" she asked, surprised to high heaven, but hoping if it was so they were fighting against the dragon fae, although she didn't want Princess Alicia involved in the mess.

"No," he said, shaking his head. "I'm merely...on vacation. So at the castle of Denkar, what is it that you do?"

She hated the question. Her brother was the one who did everything, at her mother's request. And the only time her mother gave her a job to do, it was because her brother didn't want it.

"I oversee...the servants."

Not that she really did. She oversaw her servants—all two of them—and no one else. She oversaw her brother, but he would say it wasn't true. She oversaw her cousins' misdeeds, when she caught them at it, but that was about all.

Brandolin's mouth parted slightly, then he glanced down at the medallion she wore at her throat. She noticed his was hidden. His gaze shot back up to her face. "You are royalty."

If he was King Tiernan's war minister, Brandolin would be royalty also. So why the big surprise?

"Who are your parents?" he quickly asked.

"My father has died and my mother rules."

She was pretty certain she outranked Brandolin, and she thought it was important to let him know that, just so that he knew where she stood.

His eyes took on a speculative gleam.

She ignored the uneasy sensation that slipped through her blood and gave a fake sigh. "I didn't mean to take a trip this far from home. Bye," she said quickly, then transported. Only this time she went home to do her duty, whatever that would entail. She knew he couldn't follow her there. At least he couldn't transport inside her castle or reach her bedchambers.

She headed down the corridor to see what horrible task her mother wished her to do. So much for wanting a day of danger and adventure. It seemed she needed her cousins or brother if she was going to get herself into real trouble.

Maybe later, she would try this again, without a hawk fae—who was on vacation—tracking her down.

3

Quickly, albeit reluctantly, Ritasia joined her mother in the throne room, a fire blazing at the hearth, though a chill still permeated the air and her mother's look made the room that much chillier. She was standing stiffly in front of her gold throne, which was never a good sign. If the queen sat down, she might still be tense, but when she stood, whatever she had to say was vitally important to her. Standing gave her more power to her speech before her minions. Right now, Ritasia was as much a minion as anyone else in the lion fae kingdom.

"Where have you been? I summoned you over an hour ago." Queen Irenis waved her hand dismissively, not really wanting to hear Ritasia's excuse. "After one of our fae tried to steal an artifact from the ancient digs at Calus, who remains in the dungeon, you will serve as my representative at the site. Deveron has enough on his plate to manage."

So this was what her mother had come up with. Deveron might have had enough to do already, but Ritasia was certain he wouldn't have wanted this assignment. There was no changing her mother's mind in this. Once her mother gave an assignment to one of her royal offspring, she was determined to see it through.

But what female royal fae would be in the least bit interested in mucking about in the dry, dusty dirt, or when it rained, the wet, muddy dirt, looking for old stuff that didn't matter one iota?

So some ancient Denkar fae queen wore an ivory comb encrusted with emeralds in her long hair. So what?

She wondered if this had more to do with her getting into a spat with the unseelie fae.

"Couldn't Micala or Niall have the job?" Ritasia asked, trying not to sound as irritated as she felt. "I'm sure I heard Micala say something about how fascinated he was concerning an earlier find this year. A clay pot full of very old herbs? The plants no longer in existence? Or Niall. He was really intrigued with the finding of that ancient queen's comb."

"Really?" Ritasia's mother said, but the dark look in her nearly black eyes meant she didn't believe Ritasia one little bit. Worse, she wasn't changing her mind about what Ritasia was tasked to do.

Instead, the queen continued, "You will catalog every item or ensure the cataloguer is properly listing and annotating details about every find, and then you will sign the document, verifying its authenticity. Once the treasures have been removed from the digs to the vault, you will again verify that each item is secure in its proper place."

Well, Ritasia supposed she could do that once a month. She didn't believe that many relics were found on a weekly basis. This could be doable.

"You will visit the current site of excavation twice a day. I will leave it for you to decide as to the times of day."

Ritasia barely suppressed a groan. She figured her mother would have spies reporting whether she showed up the two times a day, at least for a while. "But..."

"My mind is made up, Ritasia. Do this or I'll be compelled to find you another task that you might like even less."

Ritasia wanted to know what other task her mother might come up with, just in case she really didn't mind it as much as this one. But she was afraid to ask, knowing her mother might add it to the other, and then she would have to do both. She suspected this truly did have something to do with Ritasia's mincing words with the unseelie. It was a good thing her mother didn't know about her trying to fly somewhere else for the day.

"This will keep you out of trouble and perhaps deter some unscrupulous fae from trying to pilfer from our ancient heritage again."

Ancient heritage? Since when did old discarded fae junk equate to something as profound as *their heritage*?

"You might as well run along and check on the site now. Malathon is awaiting your verification of his note-taking."

"So, I'm supposed to check out all the sites?" Ritasia smiled faintly. "The site at Antaris? Keleron? The caves at Omonton?"

Ritasia had only been to those three sites, though close to twenty were supposed to exist. At least according to ancient documents.

She'd visited Antaris because her brother, Deveron, and cousins, Micala and Niall, had teased her that she would be afraid to see the site. Ghosts were reputed to plague the location, but she'd never seen them or sensed them there. All she remembered of the site was that dwellings had been carved high into cliffs, and the archeologists there hadn't liked that she was climbing on the flimsy ladders. They figured her cousins and brother could manage well enough. Although she didn't know what all the fuss was about. Her mother had once said she was more like a mountain goat than a princess when she'd caught Ritasia climbing a counter to reach a jar of sugared candy.

Ritasia had visited Keleron also. Again, goaded on by her brother and cousins because they dared she would not be able to face the draw of the partial buildings unearthed and the magnificent murals painted on marble walls within.

She remembered them as being dirty, the brilliant colors, if the colors had even been brilliant at one time, being leeched out by years of having been buried under tons of red clay. Unless she could observe the items in their present glory, she just didn't have the ability to see the beauty in such a thing. Old was old. And that was all there was to it.

The third visit to an archeological dig, and the absolute last, was to the underwater caves at Omonton. This one had been much more dangerous to navigate, and if her mother had known Deveron and his cousins had goaded her into visiting the cave, they would have all been in really big trouble. Even the fae who were digging there at the time looked horrified to see so many of the royals appear there when it had been deemed strictly off-limits to all but the cavers and archeologists who knew what they were doing.

Even so, several of the professional archeologists and cavers had died over the years excavating the site as the sea was known to fill the cave without warning, trapping, and drowning the unsuspecting.

Still, Ritasia had not needed as much of a prod to check out this dig. Whatever was forbidden fascinated her much more. Such was the way of the fae.

But the site had been like all the rest. Old stone carvings, stone pillars and engravings, all that indicated some ancient fae civilization had long ago lived here.

The sea hadn't even risen to make the trek more interesting. A wasted day, as far as she had been concerned.

She had never been interested in old stuff, the digging fervently in the dirt for what? Some hint of the past life some fae had lived? Who cared?

"No, not any of the sites you mentioned." Her mother gave her a sly look. "You will only be at Calus because it is the most active of the digs and has proven to carry some nice artifacts. I don't want to see any of them come up missing."

They were already missing, for goddess sakes. What difference would a few more centuries make?

No matter how Ritasia tried to view the search for relics, she could not understand how important any of this could be. "Are... you looking for anything in particular, my lady mother?" Ritasia asked.

She had only asked, trying to figure out why her mother was even vaguely interested in the sites. Her mother responded in the negative so quickly Ritasia suspected she was indeed searching for something special. Valuable? Or something more than valuable?

Now this was much more intriguing! Would Malathon know what her mother was searching for? If the cataloger did not know, then would one of the archeologists?

Was that the reason the finding of the ancient queen's comb was so important? Because she had once held some treasure and now her mother wanted it?

If that was so, what was the treasure?

Ritasia stiffened and put on her best serious face, trying not to look intrigued. "I will do as you bid and must be off now before too much more of the day passes."

"Aye. Twice a day, mind you." Then her mother dismissed her and Ritasia hurried off to change before she went to Calus, wanting to learn just what her mother wished to find at the dig and how important the item really was.

TODAY, when Ritasia reached Calus, which was nearer the sphinx fae major kingdom than the lion fae kingdom—although since the sphinx were the most acquiescent of the fae kingdoms, the Denkar had laid claim to the dig—a cool mist cloaked the area in a blanket of white, the first day it had not been sunny in the two weeks since she'd been coming here.

She loved the mist that made the whole area look surreal, fae-like, the fir trees at the edge of the dig a misty blue green, their limbs heavy with dew and in another direction, the ocean, though she could not see it this day. But she loved the sound of it as the waves crashed against the cliffs and rocky shore, the way it dragged tiny pebbles out and tossed them back again, making them smooth as glass. The way it was so secretly hidden from view while it continued to lure the visitor with its compelling draw. She loved the wet, clean smell of the air.

She gathered the mist about her, cloaked herself in it, disappearing as if she was part of the mist, thinking how the earth here was very much like it, blanketing the area so that the viewer could not see what was just located a few feet beneath it. Then she pushed away the mist and sighed. She had a job to do, as disagreeable as it was.

She glanced around at the site.

The excavated red clay had been torn away as if a wind devil had been used on the site, whipping away the earth, leaving cuts intrusively deep in some areas, shallower where ancient stone floors or pillars were laid bare. It seemed irreverent to poke and prod the area where another fae kingdom had once flourished. Almost disrespectful, like overturning headstones in a cemetery and digging around to see who lay beneath the ground.

Ritasia thought of the winged fae, Princess Serena, and how she could probably call on her wind elemental powers and forgo shovels and soft brushes to locate the valuable artifacts. Or at least those that Ritasia's mother deemed valuable.

Ritasia glanced around at the pillars, some rising twenty feet or more, some in pieces strewn all over the ground like fallen giants.

She'd heard the men commenting low to each other about how they thought a warlock, or a group of warlocks had laid siege to the kingdom long ago. But they needed proof that it hadn't been just some fate of nature, which brought the kingdom tumbling to its knees.

Several ancient sites were known to exist in the dark fae realm of the Denkar, but no one knew what had happened to the ancient fae civilizations or why they had all vanished. Although some suspected it had to do with the fight between fae that had broken the courts into the unseelie and seelie, their kingdoms forever separated by a protective invisible barrier.

Nothing in the excavations had yielded anything of interest to Ritasia. Not the unique baubles or invaluable gems, or the moldy, dusty leather-bound books of some ancient era, filled with writing no one could decipher. Not that she didn't have things she had loved since the time when she was little that she treasured as much as she was sure the fae living in these sites had once cherished their own simple treasures. When she was gone, she was certain her possessions would interest no one, but curious archeologists in some distant future.

The way they would feel about her old things would not be the same as she did. Wasn't it true that the memories connected with the item was what made it so special? Not the object itself, particularly. So future finders would not know the memories associated with such an item.

Four men were gingerly digging in one area of the site, and she walked over to join them. The air was heavy with chilly moisture. Only torchlight highlighted the thick mist, though a ray of sun was attempting to break through some of it. She stared at the ground coated in a layer of wet dirt, just like she figured it would be. Everything was light orange red, the sides of the excavation, the pillars, the ground. Nearby, six pillars lay on their side in the red clay. A grouping of four of them stood beyond them like vigilant soldiers watching over the ancient castle that once stood here, somehow withstanding the shifting earth, or whatever else had forced them to fall.

She followed Malathon around as he catalogued some of the items. He was garbed in brown robes because he was a scholarly type. In fact, all the archaeologists here were.

She, on the other hand, wore leggings that were great for climbing over fallen pillars and into excavated pits. The tunic was form-fitting enough so that the garment wouldn't catch on jagged rocks or timber. Her dark hair was still coiled about her head and tucked under a dusty hat that was half hiding her face. The hat looked like one of those Australian outback kinds with ties to keep it snug while the chilly breeze blew across the dig site. Even her brown leather boots were covered in a couple of layers of wet, red dust.

She didn't mind getting dirty, if it was for a good cause. But this? This was a total waste of time.

For two weeks, she had returned to the site for her obligatory two visits per day. Today, again, she'd needled Malathon about whatever Mother wished to find, but if he knew, he wouldn't tell Ritasia. Malathon stroked his short blond beard as he observed one of the men brushing off a...

Ritasia drew closer. Arm bone? Yuck.

She hadn't thought they would begin to find body parts. How gross! So much for discovering treasure that her mother thought would be really important. She moved away from the site and cast a glance in the direction of the forest. She swore a glint of something caught a ray of sunlight that spilled through the clouds and mist.

She stared at the forest where she was sure she saw something shiny, unnatural in the cloak of green woods—a tiny shaft of sunlight on metal. She thought.

"Princess!" Malathon snapped, drawing her attention. "Stay close."

She looked sharply at him, surprised at the warning in his voice. She wasn't *that* far from the dig. Had he seen something in the forest that had worried him?

"Did you see anything in the woods?" she asked.

"Trees. Just don't wander off."

She stared again at the shadowed trees, thinking one of the shadows moved, but then she was certain her eyes were playing tricks on her. But she couldn't budge from the spot as she waited for anything—another movement other than the heavy fir branches waving in the cold twisting breeze, to see if there truly was something that wasn't tree-like, moving through the forest.

She'd been warned time and again that the dragon fae, Duke Tully, would materialize just about anywhere with his band of merry hostage takers and grab royals as he made a living at receiving ransoms for high-ranking persons, as long as the ruling monarch wished the ranked person returned. She wondered what the duke would do if he took a hostage, and no one wished to pay a ransom.

He was considered to be a Robin Hood of sorts, taking from the rich and giving to the poor. Although from what she understood, he never took a dragon fae royal hostage. It wouldn't do to anger his own king. And he kept enough of his ransoms for himself to make a decent wage.

It was said that those who were poor, if they spied him in their neck of the woods, didn't report him either, most likely believing he might share his treasure with them as well.

Even those faced with being taken hostage had to admire the man's crass and cunning. If they could avoid being captured, they would do whatever it took. But he was said to treat his hostages in the most hospitable way and so, though the rulers of the region wished to incarcerate him in the dankest dungeon, none wished to end his life—permanently.

She'd heard tales he was a handsome man, well-liked by

everyone from the men who rode with him, to those he captured, and she wished she could meet him in person. Not to be his prisoner, of course. But to see if all the stories she'd heard were true, or if they were just tales that had been embellished to lead the listener on.

She even wondered if he ever fell in love with a high-ranked female, as he was as just about as highly ranked as they come, if he would give up his hostage-taking pursuits. Or would the lady be like him? And help him in his cause?

Such were the thoughts swirling around her brain when she saw a glint of a sword. It wasn't her imagination. A man was watching them—or maybe her alone—from the distant woods.

In an instant, one of the palace guards appeared next to her and quickly said, "'Tis time to return to the castle."

That's when she noted one of the archeologists had vanished, then he suddenly reappeared, looking steadily at her, his expression stern.

"Yes, go, Princess Ritasia," Malathon said. "You can return later in the day."

Before she could respond, an army of a dozen castle guards appeared and headed straight for the woods.

Malathon *had* seen someone in the woods but hadn't wished to alarm her. Yet he must have believed if she remained here while he sent one of his men back for a castle guard and more men to track him, the villain would continue to skulk in the woods, watching her. Waiting for a chance to grab her.

She didn't want to go now. More than anything, she wanted to follow the guards into the woods and see if they captured whoever had been lurking there.

"I will stay until the men return." She folded her arms and looked as imperious as any princess could look who wished her way in some matter.

"But Princess..."

She frowned at Malathon. "My mother wished me here. Whosoever it is would not be so foolhardy to come this way, not when he is being chased by dark fae knights."

"If it is Duke Tully, it is rumored that he can vanish and reappear anywhere so quickly that no one could react in time. What if he was to appear beside you, seize your arm, and fae transport you far away?"

"Fish tales," she said. "Besides, what if it isn't even him?"

"Even worse. Then we would have no idea what the man was up to or what his abilities would be."

"I'm not going." She motioned to the digs. "You can return to work. I have my bodyguard. I'm fine."

"Your mother would have my head if anything untoward should happen to you." But Malathon didn't order the guard to return her. And she suspected he had his reasons, but she wasn't privy to them.

Instead, both he and the guard stood beside her while the other men returned to their work, casting glances in the direction of the forest while Ritasia kept her eyes mostly on the woods.

"Could it have been a thief?" Ritasia finally asked, after they'd been standing in the same spot for half an hour, maintaining the same diligent observation of the woods.

"Possibly. He might have been wondering if we were finding anything of import here. The fact that one man has tried to steal from the dig site already and now that the queen herself wishes you to check on the excavation twice daily might give thieves ideas."

She wanted to tell him that perhaps she shouldn't be here but bit her tongue. What was here that anyone, particularly her mother, would be interested in? A magical scepter? Or some other magical artifact?

Most fae had special abilities of their own so most didn't need any magical tools. Some created magical artifacts. Some were said to have been brought to their world by creatures not fae. Although others said it was the stuff of fairytales. That no one was here before the fae.

Another hour passed before the knights returned, the red-bearded one in charge, Sir Conklin, shaking his head to Malathon. Then he spoke to Ritasia, "My lady, I thought you would have already returned to the castle."

"I wished to remain here," she said, sweeping her hand toward the site, "doing my duty to the queen."

Sir Conklin didn't even attempt to hide a knowing grin. "I dare say, my lady, you wished to know who we caught before you left the site."

"You wound me, Sir Knight. You think I would neglect my duty?"

"I believe you wished to join us on the hunt. Are you leaving anytime soon?"

She glanced back at the woods, then shook her head.

He motioned to his men to take positions around the perimeter. "By all means, do your duty then."

As if she truly wanted to stay here for the rest of the day. "Will he return?" she asked.

"They were on horseback and left the area before we reached them."

"They?" That made her think again that it was Duke Tully. "Did they leave a trail?"

"No. And I needed to ensure that you were still safe."

"How many were there? Was it Duke Tully and his men?"

"We found evidence of five horses. It might have been Duke Tully," Sir Conklin said. "I must see to my men and their place-ment." He bowed low to her and then hurried off to speak with his knights, one of whom he returned to the castle, no doubt with word to her mother about the unwelcome visitors to the site and what they had learned. And to say the princess was staying here to do her duty.

She was somewhat surprised that no one came from the castle, insisting that she return home, but it was only late afternoon. She decided to hang around longer, hoping whoever had come by to watch them, might try again.

This time maybe her men would catch them.

4

King Tiernan enjoyed feasting with the sphinx king, King Persenus and his son, Prince Raglan, late that afternoon, who looked similarly to his father, dark brown eyes and hair, powerful, broad shoulders and tall stature, but his father's hair was peppered with gray. Both were dressed to impress the hawk fae king, wearing blue velvet tunics trimmed in gold. But Tiernan was curious as to who the maiden in the tunic and breeches had been at the excavation site. If she was one of the sphinx fae, he wished to meet her, but he hadn't seen any sign of her in the great hall at the feast. And he'd looked.

So had his men, knowing just who he sought to locate.

Fascinated, he and his advisor and other men had watched her climbing over pillars and disappearing into trenches at the dig. He hadn't planned to leave the area until a man in charge of the site became wary and called the guard. Which made him suspect she must be someone important. Or they were just concerned Tiernan and his men had planned to steal from the site.

Not wishing a confrontation, Tiernan and his men had found their way to the sphinx fae court, where he assumed that the ruler, King Persenus, owned the land. He felt it refreshing to see a female fae who was so enthusiastic about such an unusual job for a woman. He'd never heard of a female archeologist, but he thought the notion quite novel. Did the kingdom here have warrior women also?

He finished eating his fowl and took another swig of his wine. "We chanced upon your dig site some miles from here," he said, cautiously, not wanting the king to believe he had any plans to lay claim to anything there.

"At Calus?" Persenus said. "The dark fae own the site. Queen Irenis, their ruler, has been most interested in the finds there. Though I have heard she has found nothing of real significance except that an ancient queen named Minova ruled there. She was thought only to be of myths and legends, but now it seems the stories hold a bit of truth after all."

The hawk fae had their own sites that Tiernan's people were excavating, trying to learn more of the history of the fae who lived in ancient times. He'd been intrigued with the past history. How peaceful they could be. And how warlike, too.

"I saw a young woman at the site—"

"Beg your forgiveness for saying so," King Persenus said, "but women would never be at the site. Not unless it was Queen Irenis herself. And I've never heard that she would visit there, unless her archeologists made a significant find."

King Tiernan leaned back in his chair and studied the sincerity of the sphinx king. "A woman *was* at the site."

"Well," Persenus said, "someone tried to steal from the place a few weeks ago. I wonder if the queen has sent her daughter to watch over the site. Although I would have thought Prince Deveron or one of their male cousins would have been given the assignment. The digs are no place for a young lady."

Prince Ragland smiled in a conceited way and raised his goblet of wine. "Sometimes the princess is just as rough and tumble as her brother and male cousins."

"Oh?" King Tiernan asked, his interest even more piqued.

"Aye. A few weeks ago she created quite a stir. She was found trespassing against the dragon fae and was tossed into their dungeon."

Instantly annoyed with the notion, Tiernan straightened. "Really."

"Oh, aye, and Queen Irenis was ready to go to war to be sure."

If Tiernan had known of the incident, he would have been also.

"The two kingdoms have never gotten along. I've thought of offering for her myself, the princess, that is, though she would be a lot to handle," Prince Ragland said, puffing his chest out with pride.

The woman sounded even more intriguing than Tiernan had at first thought. King Tiernan's advisor smiled at him, and Tiernan suspected he had not hidden his interest sufficiently from those gathered at the feast.

Seeing Tiernan's expression, Prince Ragland quickly said, "But she has turned down twenty-five suitors already, her brother has told me."

Was the prince afraid she would reject him also? That was why he hadn't asked to court her?

"She doesn't wish to marry anyone at present," Prince Ragland added, as if he needed to emphasize the point.

"The wish would be that of her mother's," Tiernan said coolly.

Ragland glanced at his father whose brows were arched in surprise. The prince added, "She is quite fond of the area. She never leaves."

"Except to visit the dragon fae in their dungeon?" Tiernan said, the undercurrent of anger in his voice evident, as he thought to wage war on the dragon fae he didn't even know. Placing a princess from another kingdom in a dungeon went beyond decorum.

"Prince Deveron, her brother, encourages her wildness at times. She often tries to get him out of the trouble he gets himself into, which causes her to get into just as much trouble," the prince said, sounding annoyed.

"She is an innocent then?" King Tiernan asked, one brow raised, suspecting she was not.

"If it wasn't for her brother, aye. And her cousins also."

"What does she enjoy doing when she is not saving her brother and cousins from ruin?"

Ragland frowned at Tiernan. "She spends her time with the ladies of the court, singing and doing needlepoint. That sort of thing. Like any high ranked lady of a court should."

"And when she isn't doing that sort of thing, she's climbing over pillars at an ancient site," King Tiernan remarked.

Ragland's frown deepened and his voice took on an annoyed tone. "She doesn't like them. Her mother must have forced her to work there."

"Really?"

"Aye. Her brother teased her into going to three other sites with him and their cousins last year. Before this, she had no interest in seeing them. He told me how easy it is to dare her."

At that, King Tiernan couldn't help smiling. The woman sounded perfectly willful, and he loved a challenge. Yet, when he recalled the way she was climbing around the dig, he didn't believe she looked to have hated being there.

"We would have you stay for as long as you wish for jousting, feasts, hunting in the forests, whatever you desire," King Persenus said.

"I must apologize," Tiernan said, shaking his head, "but I cannot stay away from my own duties for too long."

"Then you are here because?" the sphinx king asked.

"I'm seeking a bride."

Prince Ragland's face reddened. "Do you not have any fair maidens in your own lands, King Tiernan?"

Tiernan studied the man for a moment, amused, despite the

angry way the prince had spoken to him, a hawk fae king, a guest of his father's even. "Oh, aye. But it would not do to overlook those in yours. And so with great regret, I must away to meet with Queen Irenis."

"She will say no." Prince Ragland folded his arms, his expression a scowl.

"The queen?"

"Princess Ritasia," Ragland clarified, sounding even more irritated.

"Ah," King Tiernan said abruptly. "'Tis only the queen's word that matters."

King Persenus gave his son a scolding look. "Then we will wish for your success, King Tiernan."

But Prince Ragland looked as though he would like to skewer Tiernan on a long sword, when these people were supposed to be the most peaceful of fae.

"Thank you for your generosity. Could you point us in the direction of the lion fae kingdom?" Tiernan asked.

King Persenus said, "Six hours west of here, traveling by horseback. You should be in time for supper when you arrive." He gave Tiernan a smile.

Tiernan and King Persenus rose, as did all the courtiers.

Tiernan overheard Ragland say to his father in a hushed voice, "What if I wanted Ritasia for my wife?"

Persenus said, "You must make it known to her that you are interested. This is the first I have heard of it."

Before Tiernan could take his leave, Prince Ragland stalked out of the great hall. Tiernan assumed he was on his way to inform Princess Ritasia that a foreign king wanted her hand in marriage, and maybe that Ragland wished to have it instead.

Not that Tiernan was fully decided on desiring the princess. He had not seen the woman up close, and he needed to know her better than that. They might not suit at all.

But he was intrigued, more so than he'd been with any other woman in weeks.

"Do you think she might be the one?" Lord Srenton asked King Tiernan as they rode their rented horses beyond the castle gates. His advisor sounded hopeful, probably tired of how choosey Tiernan could be.

But he intended to keep his wife forever and so he wanted one that he would enjoy spending time with as much as possible.

"She's a possibility."

"Prince Ragland seemed to be interested in the young lady."

"One must do more than take interest," King Tiernan said. "One must act." And if she was the one for him, he wouldn't hesitate to take the princess home as his bride.

Looking as unruffled as ever, Lord Brandolin, his war minister, who had separated from them to look elsewhere for a possible bride choice, headed for them from the direction of the dig site and hailed them. "I have found one who might appeal to you, King Tiernan."

"Aye? Who is this winsome maid?" he asked, most interested in what the duke had to say. He hadn't thought to bring him along on this trip at first, although he had a way with the ladies, so Tiernan thought he might be useful.

"She is a most intriguing girl, and the daughter of the dark fae queen."

Tiernan sat taller in his saddle. The girl scrambling around the dig site? "What do you know of her?" he asked, frowning.

"She was making an escape from her castle, intending to fly somewhere else from the airport in Dallas, when I had just arrived, intending to join you. But intrigued, I began following her."

Tiernan wondered if Brandolin had been fascinated in the dark fae for himself. He wouldn't have put it past him.

"She is beautiful, soft hair nearly midnight in color, large eyes a pretty green, and ivory skin like the petals of the lily, and she wore a fragrance of jasmine. But 'tis her willfulness that I enjoyed the most. And her resourcefulness. When she found me following her, she quickly transported to catch another flight. Only this time 'twas to Scotland."

"Scotland, you say?"

"Aye. Only she did not plan to travel that far away from home. I unsettled her, and she found another plane to board without looking to see where it was headed."

"But we saw her at an archeological dig site."

"Really? Well, I followed her to the Denkar Castle, then ran into our minister of finance near here, scouting out the area, and he said you were dining with the king of the sphinx fae. So here I am. To give you the news."

Princess Ritasia might very well do.

AFTER A DAY at the digs and seeing nothing of interest, and no sign of the men who had been watching them earlier, Ritasia was about ready to leave. Well, past ready to leave. But she still had hoped they would find something that might have made the day worthwhile.

That's when she spied what looked to be a rusty hinge mostly buried in the dirt. Barely an outline of one tiny edge of it caught her eye. Which was why no one else had seen it yet. Besides that everyone else was working on the other side of the site.

She was headed for it when Malathon said, "The sun is setting, Princess Ritasia. Queen Irenis would not want you out this late at night and the evening meal is no doubt ready to be served."

She eyed the rusty hinge, wanting to secure the box before she had to leave the site, but she wanted to know what was in it before she had to give it up to anyone.

Which meant?

She had to return when no one was about. Later. Tonight.

But still, she wanted to stay just a few more minutes. Try to bury it a bit so no one else might catch sight of it.

Malathon surely had to be jesting that she had to be home by a certain hour. Just a few weeks ago she'd slept at the Texas Renaissance fairgrounds all night long and no one had even learned she was missing.

Well, not until the next day when word reached her mother that she was in the dragon fae dungeon. But if it hadn't been for that, she would never have been missed.

"I'll be fine," she said. "I just want to look around a little more." She didn't want Malathon to see her checking on the hinge, in case she could make some really neat discovery all on her own. He wasn't leaving her alone though. Well, in fact, no one was. Even the knights guarding her turned to watch her as if they might be needed to forcibly escort her home.

"Your mother would have me clamped in fae irons, Princess. Come, we will return now. I hadn't realized how late it was getting. The meal will soon be served," he again reminded her.

Grinding her teeth, Ritasia tried to think of a way she could stay just a little longer, but the recorder shook his head as if telling her whatever argument she wished to present wouldn't work. He wasn't letting her stay.

"Fine," she said, and stalked off. Either she would return later tonight, when everyone was busy getting ready for bed, or she would go really early in the morning before any fae—or at least the archeologists—were awake.

But as soon as she fae transported back to the castle, she remembered her mother had insisted she ensure that every ancient artifact from a half-rotted golden sandal to a broken piece of ruby-colored glass, were stored safely in the vault. Thank the goddess they had not brought the arm bone with them. Or at least they had not brought it here to be included in the treasure vault. She might be stuck with the job, but she would do as she was told. How would it look to others if she didn't? She didn't wish to set a poor example.

But still. Twenty-one useless pieces of junk had been added to the other junk. The ivory comb studded with gems sparkled in the candlelight discovered last week, and she picked up the comb and examined it more closely.

A dark strand of hair was twisted around the teeth of the comb, and Ritasia stared at it before Deveron stalked into the vault and said, "Are you coming to dinner?"

She jumped, startled at her brother's sudden appearance and his deviously cheerful voice.

She was certain he was delighted *she* got the job of verifying the recording of the artifacts instead of him. He was wearing his royal blue uniform, gold braid all over it, and she assumed he was so dressed because he was trying to make an impression on the dragon fae princess, Alicia.

"Are you?" he asked again.

"Yes, yes. I'll be right down."

"*Now*, mother says. You are already *way* too late."

"Go away, Deveron. I'm doing the job Mother wanted me to do. If I miss the meal, I can eat in my chambers."

"She won't like it unless you're sick."

Ritasia stuck the ancient comb in her leather pouch.

Deveron's eyes widened. "You cannot remove artifacts from the vault. You're only to ensure they get there and stay there."

"I'm going to try and clean up the gems and see if they are brilliant or of such a poor cut that they won't shine at all. Surely the dirt on them isn't valuable."

"All right. Come on." He took her arm and pulled her out of the vault, then locked it. "If I have to eat dinner with Mother, you have to."

This time Ritasia widened her eyes. "Why? What's wrong now?"

"More of a case of who's coming to dinner."

"Who's coming to dinner?"

Deveron grimaced when he looked at her, but he didn't say.

She slugged him. "Who, Deveron?" Then she got a really bad feeling about this. "Not that arrogant Duke Feneroal from the sphinx fae kingdom, is it? I thought we'd ruined his visit to such a degree he would never come back."

Deveron smiled.

"Unless he has returned to get even. Micala and Niall might have gone a bit too far."

"Our cousins?" Deveron snorted. "You're the one that slipped the sleeping powder into his wine, making him fall fast asleep in his pudding. Talk about shocked courtiers. Not to mention Mother. Luckily, he didn't suffocate in the stuff."

"I didn't expect him to pass out. Well? Is it him?"

"No, not him."

"Who then?"

"Someone I've never seen before, but he wants Mother to allow him to court you."

She rolled her eyes. Fifth fae in a week.

"And Prince Raglan was here earlier, looking for you, all in quite a state. He wouldn't tell me what it was all about, and then Mother learned he was there, she took him to task, though I still don't know what was going on, and sent him back to his own kingdom."

Ritasia frowned at her brother. "Whatever did he want?"

Deveron shrugged. "I have no idea." Then he gave Ritasia an accusing look. "You're not intending to pull any shenanigans at dinner with this potential suitor, too, are you? Mother said she wouldn't tolerate it."

"As if I'm the only one who pulls them. Between you and our cousins…speaking of which, where is Micala? He'd better not be with that human girl, Cassie, or Mother will be furious. She might even make him do the job she has assigned to me."

"I highly doubt it. She has told me she's much pleased with the way you've been so dedicated to your job. She only wishes she had tasked you to do it earlier on."

Ritasia hmpfed under her breath. Then she wondered why Deveron had come for her when she thought Alicia was making a special guest appearance at dinner, and he would have been too busy visiting with her. "Has Alicia not arrived yet?"

Deveron didn't say anything, but his expression darkened.

"She's not coming," Ritasia guessed aloud. "Why? Because she's mad at you for not making Micala stop dating her friend Cassie?"

"There's nothing wrong in it as long as neither of them make a big deal of it. And no one catches them at it."

Ritasia stared at her brother in shock. How could he say such a thing? "Of course there is. And you know it. A human is no match for a fae. Mother forbids long-term engagements between our people and theirs."

"I've talked to Micala again. All right?"

"And?"

Deveron shrugged.

"Well, I've talked to him also. But he rarely listens to me. What about having Mother speak with him?"

"I don't *dare* tell her."

"Why not? Surely she would set him straight before this really gets out of hand." Ritasia saw the worried look on her brother's face. "What?" Then she frowned. "No. She wouldn't."

"Aye, Mother might. One human girl is of no consequence."

"Maybe not to most fae. But Alicia would be angered beyond reason if Mother should even think of eliminating Cassie. And she probably would be mad at you, too."

"Yeah, well, don't tell Mother."

Ritasia gave her brother a sour look. "As if I would want the human girl's death on my hands. And Alicia happens to be my friend, you know. So I totally sympathize with her. I like Cassie also, the truth be known." Then she frowned at her brother. "So who is this dinner guest?"

"One of the hawk fae from halfway around the world."

Ritasia stared at her brother. "We know very little about them. Almost nothing in fact." Then she frowned, recalling the one she had met on the plane. "The war minister from the hawk fae kingdom?"

"Who?" He shook his head. "Mother wants you to get to know him. She has all kinds of getting-to-know-each-other activities planned for the two of you."

"When I said no to the other twenty-five, she dropped them as possible suitors. Why not this time?"

"He's a king."

Ritasia pulled her brother to a full stop in the hallway outside the great hall where everyone was gathering for dinner and cheerful conversation filled the room. "How old is he?" If it was the war minister for the king, he was her age and handsome. But the king? She was thinking ancient, like Alicia's grandfather who ruled over the dragon fae. Or Prince Raglan's father who was middle-aged, for the fae, and set in his ways. Although he was seeing a fae who was not much older than Ritasia. A shudder ran through her body.

"Not much older than you. He has just taken over upon his father's death. And he needs a queen to rule alongside him."

"Why consider me? Why not someone from his kingdom or one of the closer fae kingdoms? Is he an ogre? Everyone knows the truth about him for miles around so he has to come all this way to find an acceptable bride?" She shook her head. "It's on the other side of the world. I don't want to live that far away."

"It's not exactly on the other side of the world. And Mother wants you to seriously consider him."

Ritasia wouldn't. She wasn't going to leave this hemisphere for anything or anyone, even if he was a king.

Ritasia was glad she hadn't had time to change out of her dusty brown clothes that she'd worn just for going to the dig. Her mother would have a fit. Deveron, typical brother, never even noticed or he would have insisted she change before arriving at the great hall. Either that or he hadn't liked the king and was hoping Ritasia could discourage him in this way. No king would be interested in a princess who arrived at the supper meal wearing dusty male breeches and a tunic. How could he possibly view her as his queen? She smiled evilly.

As soon as they entered the great hall, all conversation ceased and a hush descended, making Ritasia feel suddenly self-conscious. Everyone had already taken their seats, and everyone was dressed as if they were celebrating a regal affair.

Which made Ritasia stand out even more.

When Prince Deveron and Princess Ritasia walked toward the dais, nearly everyone but the queen rose in silent greeting, bowing their heads or curtseying.

Ritasia wished more than ever that she'd taken her meal in her room.

Her mother was glowering at her. Partly, because she was late. But also because of the way she was dressed.

Ritasia was not at fault that her mother had given her this job to do. The work took longer than she'd expected. And her mother hadn't given her time to change clothes either. Well, Deveron hadn't.

Ritasia stood straighter and headed for her seat at the high table, then saw that a man was seated in *her* chair. "Why is that man sitting in my chair?"

"*That* is the king. He has a Celtic human kind of name that means regal."

"Is he? Or just some barbarian king? Or something else..." She let her words trail off as she studied the king, his posture, leaning forward at the table, interested.

Wavy light brown hair and smiling blue eyes caught her attention. She wasn't certain if he was amused in a way that said she looked comical to him—especially the way she was dressed, or if he liked what he saw. She decided the way his mouth curved up, that he thought she served as the jester for the court.

He was as handsome as Brandolin, his war minister, just as tall and regal.

"His name is Tiernan. And you are to behave yourself," her brother belatedly told her.

"Right."

Was he a soft ruler? One who didn't really work for a living but was more of a figurehead? Some rulers were and their advisors or counsel of advisors ruled instead. She certainly didn't want to be married to anyone like that. Not that she was even seriously considering such an arrangement. She did *not* want to leave this part of the fae globe.

"I suspect that Prince Raglan knew something of this king, came here to warn you, and wanted to be seated at the head table with us, but Mother said no and sent him away."

Ritasia sighed. "I will have to thank him for trying to save me."

From the moment she had stepped into the great hall and noticed the king, his gaze had remained fixed on her. Probably judging her grace and bearing. Well, she had no intention of behaving in whatever way he envisioned his queen should perform. Which meant she would act the way she normally did and not put on any pretentious airs.

Although as soon as she reached her seat, she hadn't quite meant to say what she did. Not with her mother looking on.

"You are sitting in *my* chair, my lord." She said the words very civilly, she thought. Although he quirked a brow and lowered his chin as if giving her one of those looks. Like really? In a way that wasn't a question. She was telling a fae king, a *hawk* fae king, and a guest of the dark fae, that he shouldn't be sitting in her seat?

But she didn't stop there. "You may sit there if it pleases you." She pointed to Micala's seat since he was not at the meal.

Her mother's mouth gaped and for once she didn't have an immediate rebuke ready for Ritasia.

The king gave Ritasia such a sinister smile, she was afraid she might have gone a little too far with her first encounter with him. She quickly remembered her manners, curtseyed, though because she wasn't wearing a gown, she thought she looked a little ridiculous, then looked back up at him.

She immediately rethought her position when she saw how much her mother was glowering daggers at her. She realized moving the king would put her right next to her mother, which was normally where she sat and that was the point she was trying to make. But it would be too difficult getting away with much mischief if she sat that close to her mother.

Before she could amend her statement, the king spoke. "I take it this is your lovely daughter, Princess Ritasia, my lady," Tiernan addressed Queen Irenis, his voice deep and appealing. Too appealing.

Ritasia wasn't sure he was being sincere in his compliment, or being facetious instead, considering the way she had treated him.

"Yes, and she will take her cousin's seat at once," Queen Irenis said. Her biting words warned Ritasia not to take her disobedience any further.

Ritasia wasn't stupid. But being the queen's daughter, she had some of her stubbornness, and the notion still irked her that she would be relegated to her cousin's chair instead of her own. She had half a mind to sit at one of the lower tables where the queen made Micala sit when he displeased her. She swore her mother could not read minds, but the queen pointed at Micala's vacated chair at the high table, as if silently warning her not to try her patience any further.

"Nay!" King Tiernan said. "If the lady feels more comfortable in her own chair, so be it."

"I'll take Micala's chair," Ritasia quickly said, curtseying to both the queen and the king, and trying not to look pleased that she had her way once she'd come to her senses. To her surprise and embarrassment, he quickly stood, pulled Micala's chair out for her, then once she was seated, her face had to be as flushed as the red clay soil at the dig as hot as it was, she sat down.

She noticed just how quiet the great hall still was as every eye was on her. And him.

He leaned down and whispered into her ear, "It won't work, you know."

His warm breath against her sensitive skin made her heart thump irregularly. She looked up at him as he towered over her, that same elusive smile playing on his mouth.

He didn't...intimidate her, exactly. But she was quickly coming to the conclusion that she couldn't...manipulate him like she could the other men who had feigned the least bit of interest in her. Which was partly the reason she wasn't interested in them in return, she belatedly realized.

Queen Irenis quickly signaled for the meal to begin as the king and Deveron—she finally noticed he'd been waiting to see what happened next, ever the protective brother and she loved him for it —took their seats and everyone else followed suit.

"I see by your clothes that you've just come from the digs. Your mother said you were verifying the finds." He had pulled her chair too close to the one he was sitting in—that was normally hers— and his leg was indecently touching hers.

But when she tried to scoot Micala's chair away, he seized the arm and shook his head. "Sit still, unless you wish to provoke your mother's ire further."

He was a *tyrant*!

She ground her teeth, then said, "Why are you here?" She figured she would get the truth out of him sooner than later.

He smiled again, but this time it was more as though she'd asked some inane question.

She continued, figuring she would have to spell it out for him. "Have you no women from where you come from who would want to marry you?"

Well, that wasn't exactly the way she meant to say it. She'd meant to be much more tactful, but when he wouldn't let her move away from him, he'd provoked *her* ire.

"Oh, aye," he said, his blue eyes darkening. "Women so beautiful, they take a man's breath away. Who are so willing to do whatever a man desires. Who…"

"Ahh, then why did you come here? You will find no woman like that here." Well, of course he would, but not when it came to her!

He grinned. "Which do you mean? Not beautiful, or…unwilling to bow to a man's wishes?"

"A doormat of a woman. Unless she is paid for her services."

Both of his brows lifted.

"A maid who works for the man. If you work for someone and he…" She didn't like the look of amusement on his face. "Never mind. We don't have the kind of women here that you seek. I'm certain my mother will ensure that you are well entertained before you leave, but—"

"Aye, she has planned several outings for us."

Ritasia's mouth dropped, but she quickly recovered. What part of she wasn't going to be included in this whole scene didn't he get?

"You cannot be serious." She didn't want to mention that she wouldn't suit him as a bride, when he might not be considering such a thing at all and laugh his head off. Maybe he was bored and thought to seek some entertainment before he returned to his kingdom of beautiful, willing women.

"I'm always, well, mostly always serious. Tonight—"

"Tonight, I'm taking a bath and retiring for the evening after the meal. My mother might have mentioned she gave me an important job to do. I have to be up early for the digs." She lifted her chin, waiting for his reaction, expecting he would get her point that she was not going to roll over and play dead and do as he wished.

"*After* we walk in the gardens."

His words were spoken so abruptly, she knew she didn't have any choice. If she could just conjure up a rainstorm, she would have it made.

"A *brief* walk," she said, just as sharply.

The smile in his expression told her she wasn't winning this game. She assumed the only way to beat him was to solicit her cousins' help. She was certain Deveron wouldn't go along with it. She wasn't sure her cousins would either. Sometimes they could get away with their shenanigans. But when it came to defying Queen Irenis, the stakes had to be high enough. And she was certain her cousins wouldn't interfere. Deveron would, if he thought Ritasia needed protection. But if he didn't, well, she would be on her own.

Then she had an idea. She smiled sweetly. "Not the gardens. How about a trip to the digs?"

He frowned. "This late at night?"

"Aye." She still wanted to see if she could find what the hinge in the ground led to.

His smile returned. "I see."

She frowned at him. What did he *see*? "There's something at the dig that I want to check out."

He instantly sobered.

What? Did he think she was so taken with him that she wanted to be alone at the dig site with him? *Please.*

"Unchaperoned?" he asked, sounding a little surprised.

For an instant, she felt a flight of butterflies take off in her stom-ach. Why did the sound of his words, the lift of his brows, the interest in his voice, cause her such anxiety? "We would not be allowed to go to the digs this late at night, with or without a chaper-one," she said brusquely, keeping her voice low, but what did he think? She could do stuff like that without consequence? That was if she got caught?

So of course she couldn't go there with a chaperone. And if she wasn't forced to, she wouldn't be taking him along either.

The woman was an imp, King Tiernan thought. He was so surprised when she had told him—*him*, the king of the hawk fae—to move from *her* chair, that she had momentarily stunned him to silence.

He couldn't remember a time when *anyone* had done that to him. Not even his father, the king, as little as he'd seen of him.

Even the queen and all her courtiers hadn't spoken a word when the princess had told him where to sit. Probably waiting to see his reaction. He couldn't even imagine what his own advisor was thinking at the time, nor the lords who served as his entourage this trip. He envisioned them holding their breaths, waiting for him to tell the haughty princess just where she should sit. As the tyrant he was supposed to be would have done.

Had he been alone with her in the great hall, he would have insisted she take her seat on her chair. Although he wouldn't have made a move to vacate it. See what kind of a response he would have gotten then. He smiled at the notion.

To prove to her that he wasn't a tyrant and to play the princess's game, he had offered her chair to her, just as she had wished, so that he could sit on her cousin's. But she had quickly changed her mind. And he was very well aware of her reasoning. If she had sat next to her mother, she would have faced the queen's wrath. Best to keep him where he was so he could act as the princess's protector.

But he had no intention of serving as her protector. He wanted very much to know everything about Ritasia before he left the region, and that included how she would react under pressure.

She barely ate any of her meal, and he wondered if he'd spoiled her appetite or if she always picked at her food.

"No appetite, my lady?"

She glanced up at him, their gazes colliding. She had the most darkly intriguing eyes, such a deep green they were nearly like jewels. Her hair was dark, tendrils having come loose beneath the goddess-awful dusty hat she wore, the straps tied around her chin, the silky strands of her hair curling over her shoulders.

"Remove your hat!" Queen Irenis snapped, her composure all but gone as she glowered at Ritasia.

The princess gave her mother an annoyed look, which amused Tiernan. The woman was a delight.

But as she tried to pull the hat free, hair pins kept it in place. She opened her mouth as if to speak, and he assumed she would tell her mother she couldn't remove her hat. But he leaned over the princess and said, "Allow me, my lady," as if he was a practiced lady's maid.

First, silence cloaked the whole of the great hall, then whispered murmurs filled the air. When he ate in the great hall in his kingdom, the place was nosier than blazes. Were the dark fae always this quiet, or was it because of his visit?

Pins scattered all over the floor as he pulled off the hat and a maid quickly rushed forth from one of the lower tables at the queen's beckoning, and the woman took the hat away.

Smudges of fine red clay dusted Ritasia's ivory cheeks, although the color rose in them again as he stared at her beauty. Dark tendrils of curls fell to her shoulders, while some of her hair was still pinned up. She was a vision—tussled, down-to-earth, simply dressed, no jewels or any kind of finery—a vision.

She quickly looked away and poked at her sweet brown bread with a knife as if seeing if the piece of the loaf was alive.

Surely other men saw just how attractive she was, and she had to be used to having men stare at her in such a way.

Tiernan caught his advisor's eye, whose questioning gaze asked if she indeed was the one. He had no idea. Not yet. Only time would tell.

"What is it you wished to see at the dig?" he whispered to Ritasia, not wishing anyone at the high table to know what they planned to do.

"Nothing much."

He stared at her, not believing a word she said. "Oh? Then why go tonight? Why not wait until tomorrow when the men are working on the dig? When it's easier to see in the daylight?"

"I will be stuck with you, if my mother has her way and you do not object."

He smiled at her, unable to help himself. "Interesting choice of words, my lady." He was so used to women being demure around him, hanging on his every word, willing to grant his every wish, he didn't expect this kind of reaction from any woman. He wasn't sure how to take her but be amused by her sauciness. "If you were not *stuck* with me, what else would you fill your day with? Needlework and singing with the ladies?"

She looked at him as if he was out of his mind. "How droll."

He had thought the sphinx fae, Prince Ragland, had not been telling the truth about the lady. He glanced around the hall. He thought the prince would have been here and would have warned the princess of the king's coming, but it appeared she was too late in arriving at the meal, and the prince was nowhere in sight.

"I would be at the digs, as is my duty," she said, fingering her bread.

He'd never seen anyone play with her food as much as she did. "I've heard it said the excavation site does not truly interest you." Although when he had watched her scrambling over the pillars, she had looked determined to do something, and she had appeared to be enjoying the day.

"Who would have told you that, my lord?"

"Prince Ragland."

"Oh."

So the prince had been telling the truth about that. "I thought he might have even been here tonight."

"My mother said he could not stay for the meal."

Tiernan smiled. So her mother wished a chance at an alliance with his kingdom instead of Prince Raglan's.

"But you have had a change of heart about the digs," Tiernan said.

She shrugged.

"Why?

She looked up at him, parted her lips as if to speak, and in that instant, he wanted more than anything in the world to press his mouth against hers, to kiss the wine staining her lips, to feel the warmth and softness that he knew would be his to enjoy if he did so. And to see and feel her reaction to him.

Now her cheeks were freshly full of color.

The women from his kingdom and beyond his realm who would have been suitable brides were afraid of him. But Ritasia— he made her blush.

He smiled. He liked the idea of having a blushing bride.

She tossed that notion out on its ear when she frowned and whispered, "'Tis none of your concern."

But where she was concerned, he was highly interested.

When the meal ended, the queen wished a word with Ritasia, and he knew she would berate her daughter, most likely for both her appearance and her performance tonight and command her to be on her best behavior from here on out.

To forestall the inevitable and rescue the lady as it suited his purpose, he offered his arm to Ritasia. "It is getting so late; can you not speak with her in the morn? I wish to walk with her in the gardens this eve."

Queen Irenis glowered at Ritasia, a look that told her to mind her manners, then she managed a smile for the king. "By all means, my lord. Enjoy your walk." But he could tell the queen would have words with Ritasia once he returned her to the castle.

Moments later, they had barely reached the wrought iron gate to the gardens surrounded by a hedge wall of tall green yew and the walk where he would learn more about the prince, when Ritasia jerked her arm free from his. Before he could react, she vanished.

Cursing his folly for not holding the minx's arm more tightly, he transported to the ruins, thinking she had to have gone there. He had a devil of a time locating her, even thinking that she might not have come here after all. He even envisioned her reclining naked in a bath in her bedchambers—which made him think of her in an entirely inappropriate way—while she would be relishing the fact that she'd outfoxed him.

If that had been the case, he was of half a mind to remove her from her chambers and force her to walk with him in the gardens, properly dressed, of course, as he had told her mother he would do. He might not be a tyrannical king, but there were limits even he would reach when it came to his patience.

Holding a fae created light with his hands, he suddenly caught a glimpse of the princess and hurried forth, wondering what she was doing, crouched in the dirt, brushing something away with her hands and realized then how fine her fingers were, delicate, so much smaller than his own.

Looking at the way she crouched there, he thought it absurd to even consider wedding such a wench who would be his future queen. And yet, he couldn't help but be drawn to her. And he was glad she was here and not sitting in a bath in her chambers trying to rile him. Although thinking of her in the bath again was his undoing.

"We were to come here together," he said darkly. "That was the agreement."

"You knew I would be here," she hastily said, still carefully brushing away the dirt, searching for something with her fingers.

Right that instant, she made him think of a willful kitten he'd had as a boy. The fae didn't often have pets, but when he was in exile, one of the washerwomen had sneaked a marmalade-colored kitten to him so that he would have someone to play with. Cook had threatened mayhem if she ever saw the clawed devil in her kitchen, yet he'd found her serving the feline warm milk on a snowy day. Fish scraps, too. As fat at his kitten had gotten, he was certain Cook wasn't the only one who had been feeding the rambunctious kitten.

Trixie had been as playful and mischievous as any fae. She talked back in her cat way when he commanded her to get off his bookshelves, or when she'd attempt to sneak a morsel of chicken off his dinner plate. She cuddled with him when she wanted warmth and affection. And she had played hide and seek, slipping under his bedcovers, and of course he'd have to play with her in response. He had not been her master, the prince, or a future king —not to her. Maybe that's why he had loved her so much.

Ritasia may not sneak food off his plate, but she was just as mischievously sneaky as Trixie had been.

"Together," he reminded her. "And if you believe you can do whatever you wish when we have an agreement, princess—" He stopped speaking when he heard a squeak and leaned down to see what she'd uncovered.

"A trapdoor," she excitedly said. And now he saw a new side of her. Enthusiastic, excited, happy. And he liked seeing her in this way as she smiled up at him, her face so radiant in the glow of their fae light. "I thought it was only a box. But it is a trapdoor."

She lifted it and dropped it on its back. "Shall we?" She motioned to the steps leading down into the inky blackness.

"We should tell your mother about this, and she'll have her archeologists—"

Ritasia didn't wait for him to finish speaking, but hurried down into the abyss, her fairy light casting shadows about her that made her appear ethereal.

"Wait up," he growled. He had not thought himself easily irked, but then again he'd never met any woman before who hadn't groveled before him, and he was finding the lady quite a challenge. "Princess," he said, seizing her arm before she got much farther away from him, "we...go...*together*."

Her gaze darted to meet his, and he got the impression he had frightened her. But only for a moment. She didn't seem the type who frightened easily.

She gave him an exaggerated curtsey and said, "Of course, my lord. Would you like to lead the way?"

"Nay," he said curtly and firmly wrapped his fingers around hers. "We stay together at all times."

He told himself he should take the lady well in hand and return her to the surface, transport her back to the castle, and speak with the queen about the discovery they had made. Then he would walk with the princess in the gardens as any royal couple might do while he was courting the lady.

But he did wish to see Ritasia as she was, not how she would be if he forced her to go along with his wishes, no matter how much more reasonable they were than hers. And seeing the beautiful fae princess in a dark rocky tunnel was somewhat intriguing. Certainly unusual. Even for him.

"What do you hope to find?" he asked, while they walked through a narrow tunnel dug deep in the earth. He suspected it had been a secret escape tunnel used by the ancient fae who had resided in the castle.

"Probably nothing down here," she said, her sweet voice echoing off the walls, the sound of dripping water somewhere nearby. The air was colder down here, and he wondered if she was warm enough. Although at least down here there was no chilly breeze.

"Then why are we here?" he asked.

"This is an adventure. Anyone can walk in the castle gardens backlit by torches, the flames wavering in the breeze. No one has probably walked down here in a hundred years or more. Even the ancient fae who lived in the castle now in ruins probably didn't have any reason to come down here for eons."

"To escape."

"Aye. Or perhaps children might have played in these tunnels. But still, it might have been centuries since any of that had happened."

"What if we get lost? No one knows we're down here."

"We can fae transport," she said easily.

He touched the rough rock wall. "If the rock is not full of iron ore."

She chewed on her bottom lip and seemed to think better of wandering through the tunnels all night long. Yet, they would surely open up somewhere to the outside, or what good would escape tunnels be if they did not?

But what if whatever movements of the earth that had left the castle in ruins had also blocked any other exit?

"You are probably right," she finally conceded. She smiled brightly, turned back the way they had come and began walking, her boots clicking on the solid rock again.

"Most likely we would not have found anything," he said, trying to reassure her, now feeling badly that he'd dampened her enthusiasm, even though she was making the effort to appear undaunted.

She smiled up at him. "I'm sure that you are right. I need a bath and will retire to bed."

They walked in silence for some time, but he felt uneasy about her change of heart. "You will not return here tonight after I leave you." He didn't ask it as a question of her because he didn't mean it as one.

"Why, my lord, why would I do that?"

"Because somehow you crossed the dragon fae's path, angering them, and landed in their dungeon. I have no idea what other foolishness you are capable of." He still couldn't get over what she'd done and what they'd done in response. Give him a moment alone with the dragon fae who had ordered such a thing, and King Tiernan would have him on his knees begging for mercy.

She stopped and gaped at him. Then she narrowed her eyes, yanked her hand free from his, and folded her arms. "Do not call me foolish when you know nothing of the circumstances, King Tiernan."

"Then enlighten me, my lady."

"Why? You have already pronounced judgment. No wonder you are here looking for a bride. I will tell you right now it will not be me."

He held back a smile. She truly was a challenge. "What if your mother wishes it?"

"She has said she will permit me to choose among my suitors."

He thought if he played his cards right, her mother would hasten to agree to allow her daughter to wed him. He was a king after all. Of a major kingdom. "And when she tires of you saying no?"

"I will find the right one someday."

"How many kings have offered for you?" He didn't know why the words spilled out of his mouth. He had not offered for her and had no attention of doing so before getting to know her better.

She turned and stormed off. "None. And it is my fervent desire that it shall stay that way."

He stalked after her and took her hand. Looking down at her, he said, "Why? Because you cannot wind me around your fingers like a strand of hair?"

And then in the dark, her face flushed and angry, he pulled her close and kissed her. Although he hadn't meant to. But she was just too appealing. Too defiant not to.

His mouth pressed softly against hers at first, his hands cupping her face, his heart thundering like hers was.

When she didn't pull away or slap his face but lightly touched his arms as if in agreement, he deepened the kiss. 'Twas nothing like he'd ever experienced—her warm soft lips brushing his, her wine-sweetened tongue tentatively touching his.

And here they were in the dark, underground with no chaperone for the lady, no way of anyone even knowing where they were. He hastily, albeit reluctantly—*very* reluctantly—pulled away, kissed her forehead, and took her hand, then began walking back to the stairs that would take them out of here.

Neither of them spoke a word, but her hand clinging to his told him all he needed to know. She was not opposed to his kissing her, and he suspected she liked it as much as he had. Well, more than liked it. Her pulse was still beating as rapidly as his was.

She had leaned against him, her heart beating as fast as a racehorse's, a puzzled expression on her face when he had forced himself to pull away. He loved how she didn't see him as a monster, how she didn't lower her lashes, well, except to fall under the spell of his kiss, but not before that. Not when he leaned down to kiss her, like some women would do, as if they had to acquiesce to his power, his rule. Instead, she had looked up at him, wide-eyed, innocent, and interested.

He thought, though since he had not done so with anyone else before so he wasn't perfectly certain, that he might be falling in love. He could easily feel that way about Ritasia when she wasn't giving him grief and returned tenderness instead. The grief was part of the package, and he rather liked her spunkiness. He didn't think he would ever find a woman who would speak her mind with him like the dark fae would. And that more than intrigued him.

After a ponderous silence, their footfalls clapping on the uneven rock floor, she finally asked, "Do you often kiss women like that?"

He smiled at her question. She wanted to know if she was special. "In dark ancient tunnels when the lady is a princess from another major kingdom, no."

"Be serious."

"I am serious." She had to know that as well as he kissed her, it was not the first time for him. But it was the first that he'd had a devil of a time breaking off the kiss. He looked down at her. She seemed deep in thought. "Do you often kiss men like that?"

Not that he thought she did. She seemed inexperienced. Willing, but unsure of herself as to what to do.

"In dark ancient tunnels where the nobleman is a king from another major kingdom, no," she said.

He laughed and his laughter bounced off the walls in a mirthful cascade of echoes. The lady was a delight. The blush returned to her cheeks.

When they reached the stairs, something seemed wrong. He felt the area closed in, the fresh air from the outside no longer sifting in from the open trapdoor. The dark enveloped them from up above and down below, except for where their fae light dispensed the blackness in a half arc in front of them. So he couldn't see the matter. But he still felt boxed in.

She squeezed his hand and whispered in a shaky voice, "We left the trapdoor open. It's now closed."

So she had sensed it also.

She was trying to hide her concern, but Tiernan knew she was frightened. Not that he wasn't worried also. He whispered, "Stay here."

He really didn't want to leave her alone at the base of the stone stairs carved into the rock in the event someone sinister was in the tunnels and might come upon her. But he didn't want to take her up the stairs to the trapdoor and move her outside if someone dangerous happened to be waiting for them topside.

"Together," she whispered, repeating his own mantra, sounding as though staying behind scared her more than facing whoever had closed the trapdoor. "I have a dagger in my boot."

He raised his brows at her. Her words brought to mind his advisor's saying that some women in other kingdoms were warrior women. But she did not look like the kind of lady who waged war. And he doubted her mother would allow her only daughter to partake in such a deadly venture. "I have a sword, but I did not wear it to the evening meal."

"No dagger either?"

"My advisor and the rest of my men carried theirs. I was attempting to appear as though I came in peace, my lady. I never thought the digs would harbor any danger for you, or I would not have allowed you to remain here."

Ritasia tugged on his hand. "Shouldn't we at least try to fae transport out of here?"

"Aye, we shall try." He drew her closer, not needing to, but wanting to. Both tried their best to travel, but it was hopeless. "Iron ore must be in the rock. Let's try the trapdoor."

He had the sickening feeling in the pit of his stomach that the door would be blocked. He had no real good reason to feel that way, but still, he did.

When he gave it a shove, it didn't budge. He tried with all his might, first his shoulder, then his back pressing against it at alternate times, but it didn't move even a fraction of an inch.

"We're trapped down here," she said, sounding like she was fighting tears. "Do you think anyone knows we're down here?"

"Possibly. Or someone just found the opening and decided to secure it until the archeologists arrive in the morning. You've had thievery here before. A guard may check the site periodically through the night. He might have even been concerned someone might fall through the opening and injure himself."

"Then we should holler for help before he leaves."

Tiernan walked her back down the steps. "Whoever blocked the trapdoor might not be one of your mother's guards."

"My mother will kill me," Ritasia said disconsolately.

"She intended to scold you tonight when I returned you after our garden walk, did she not?"

"Oh, aye. Now she will be more than furious." She looked up at him. "What if she insists we wed?"

"We will find a way out. There must be an exit that opens to the outside somewhere. Then we can return a little later than we intended, and all will be well." The notion her mother would insist they wed had appeal, but he thought it best not to address that subject for the moment.

The problem was the deeper they walked into the tunnel, the more passages they found.

"Have we been going in circles?" Ritasia finally asked, sounding thoroughly dejected after they'd walked for what seemed like hours.

"Maybe so. Give me your dagger, and I'll carve an arrow pointing in the direction we have gone and if we see it again, we'll know we've been this way before."

6

Her mother would kill her, Ritasia thought morosely again. It had been her stupid idea to discover what the hinged box meant, at least that's what she'd thought it was. Not a trapdoor. She hadn't known what to expect, except maybe to find a treasure vault and see it first before anyone else could. No matter what she'd suspected when she'd considered the door, she hadn't believed it would lead to an endless myriad of tunnels. Surely one of them would lead outside soon. But she was afraid they'd been walking in circles.

And now they were trapped inside.

Every tunnel looked like every other tunnel, no distinguishing features from one to the next. She felt like she was in one of those poorly constructed dungeon and dragons' kind of role-playing games that the humans loved so much where the artwork was repeated and none of it varied enough so that the players would find themselves lost for hours in such a maze of tunnels. At least like the ones Alicia had shown her when she took her to her human home.

The walls were dripping with water, blanketed in emerald, green moss, an occasional stalactite holding tight to the ceiling, or a stalagmite poking up from the floor. The air was cool and moist, and she shivered, feeling as though the cool wetness was beginning to seep through her clothes into the marrow of her bones. The only thing warming her up down here was Tiernan, his body pressed against her side, his arm wrapped around her waist, keeping her tight beside him, and the thought of that surprise kiss.

She was astonished when he'd taken her in hand and kissed her, then pulled away. Though she knew he was enjoying the kiss as much as she was. Which made him all the more honorable. And yet, she wouldn't have minded the kiss lasting a bit longer.

She watched as Tiernan carved an arrow into the wall, felt a little guilty that they would leave their mark down here when it didn't belong to them. That was silly, she had to tell herself. The tunnels and wreckage of the castle didn't belong to anyone, not really, not any longer. Well, except her mother had laid claim to it.

At least Tiernan could carve something in the wall to help them determine if they were walking through the same area over and over again.

She was beginning to wonder if they should attempt to return to the trapdoor. Surely someone would come there in the morning.

The morning. Ritasia would have spent the entire night with a man who was not her relation. Even though he was a king, it would not bode well for either of them.

She wasn't sure what else to do. They hadn't found even a hint of an exit, no fresh air seeping into the passageways, no outside light, though it was probably still early night. She was so tired, she could barely lift her feet to traverse the rocky floor, stumbling more often than not, and though Tiernan was making sure she stayed on her feet, his hand securely around her waist now, he had stumbled a time or two himself.

He finally pulled her to a stop. "This area has the smoothest floor that we've come across in all our travels."

Her heart lifted and she thought he was going to say he

believed they might have found a way close to the exit. Instead, he said, "We need to rest. We're both so tired we can barely walk upright any longer. Come, lie down with me and we will sleep for a bit. Surely someone, or even more than that, will be searching the tunnels in the morning."

She wasn't ready for what he did next. She thought they would sleep close to each other for warmth and safety, but not like this.

He cuddled her against his body so she wouldn't have to recline on the cold, hard floor, kissed the top of her head, and said, "Sleep, princess. We'll be out of here in no time." His voice was weary and though he tried to sound like he knew what he was talking about, he also sounded like he didn't believe in his own words either but was only trying to reassure her.

"They'll find us," she said, snuggling against his chest, listening to his heartbeat thumping beneath his royal navy tunic decorated in gold trim, now layered in a film of red dust. She realized then he must have dressed in all his finery to impress her mother, the court, and of course, Ritasia, when she had gloated about being as poorly dressed for such an affair as possible.

She sighed.

She wouldn't have done anything differently. She hadn't known him then, hadn't wished to get to know him. Now, it was different, somehow. Maybe because they'd shared an adventure, and he had *not* gotten angry with her for getting them into this mess. Her mother would have been highly pissed. Her brother would have been extremely exacerbated. Tiernan? He was trying to make the most of it, while also attempting to ensure she was not alarmed.

She realized that adversity had only brought them closer.

She prayed that her people would find them and no one else who might wish them harm, and that her mother wouldn't be as angry with her as she knew she would be as she tried to sleep.

DEVERON PACED across his sister's chamber and stopped to ask Ritasia's maid once again, "You're sure she went to the gardens with King Tiernan?"

The older woman was wringing her hands and nodded, her eyes wide and brimming with tears. "Aye. She was walking toward them with her hand in the king's, and I returned here to make down her bed. The queen herself didn't want me to watch them walking in the gardens. She said enough courtiers were enjoying the weather before it turns too cold that she would be chaperoned adequately, and she did not want us to appear as though we didn't trust him with the princess."

Deveron stalked over to the window and looked out. "Then *where* is she? Where is *he*? His men have not seen their king any more than we can find Ritasia! Which means they are together. Somewhere. I did not think she liked the king well enough to go off somewhere with him alone."

He was trying with all his might to rein in his anger and not throw the king's men in the dungeon. They were just as concerned as he was, and they seemed sincere enough that they didn't know where their king or Ritasia had disappeared to.

Melissina offered, "He could not have taken her hostage, my lord. Not if he left his men behind."

Deveron frowned at her. "True, but then what has become of them? They have both vanished!"

"Did you not hear what she was saying to the king while you sat on the other side of the princess? Mayhap they had planned a secret rendezvous."

"I would not have thought it possible. But she *was* whispering to him. Where would they have gone?"

"'Tis a mystery to me, my lord. Usually when we cannot find her, she is with you, beg pardon."

"She is *not* with me," Deveron said coldly. "She is with *him*! And we have no notion as to what sort of a man he truly is. We have very little knowledge of the hawk fae's kind. Perhaps this is their way of securing an unwilling bride!"

"Oh, my heavens, no," Melissina said. "It cannot be true."

"We have no way of learning the truth until we find them."

"What is the queen saying about this?" Melissina whispered, her voice full of dread.

"She is sleeping, thank the goddess. She sent me to have words with Ritasia about her behavior and dress tonight. The queen was feeling tired and wished for me to deal with my sister. Thank the goddess," he repeated.

His mother would have thrown the king's men in the dungeon until someone told them where the king and Ritasia had disappeared to. Worse, the sun would be up in several hours and then what would he tell his mother when they had morning meal?

He'd been searching all night for his sister...and the king. He'd questioned everyone who had been awake and awakened those who were not, barraging everyone with the same question. Where had Ritasia and the king gone?

A light tapping on his sister's chamber door made him whip around to see a middle-aged lady standing in the doorway, a cloak about her shoulders, her pale skin flushed. "My lord," she stammered. "Lord Everton and I had taken a trip to the human world and just returned to find the place in an uproar. We just received word that you were looking for Princess Ritasia and King Tiernan. They fae traveled somewhere else. They had just reached the garden gate, and we were about to approach them and curtsey and bow to them in greeting when they disappeared."

He frowned. "Did he forcibly take her somewhere?"

"Why, no, my lord. Just the opposite."

Deveron's brows rose. "*She* forcibly took him somewhere?" His voice arced in disbelief.

"Why, no, my lord. Not exactly."

"Then *what*, pray tell?"

"Well, Princess Ritasia pulled her hand from his, and she disappeared. King Tiernan's face reddened, he cursed under his breath, and then he vanished. He did not stop to solicit anyone's help in locating the lady, so we assumed he knew where she had gone."

"So he was angry that Ritasia had left him."

"Aye, my lord. He looked quite smitten with the princess. Then quite annoyed."

Deveron scowled. He still had no idea where she would have gone to. If it hadn't been that the king seemed to know just where she had disappeared, he would have assumed she had tried to escape walking with him in the gardens.

Still several more hours before the sun would be up. He had to find her before then. Their mother would have a meltdown when she learned Ritasia and the king were missing.

He stalked out of Ritasia's chambers to find the fae trackers and head them in the right direction.

"ARE you sure it was the princess?" Duke Tully asked his second in command, delighted at the prospect that he would be able to take the lady hostage, and that Queen Irenis would pay handsomely for her return.

Lords Langtry and Havetson rolled the fallen pillar segment away from the trapdoor to the ancient ruins that they'd used to block it.

"Aye," Lord Langtry said. "We came here to see if we could find any valuable relics and saw the princess still dressed as she was earlier at the site. I have no idea who the man was that came with her here. No doubt some suitor. But she did not have a lady's maid with her so she was not properly chaperoned."

Not believing the queen would permit such behavior, Duke Tully shook his head.

"No doubt the man was highborn, at least from the way he was so elegantly dressed and would bring just as worthy a ransom. Whereas she was dressed in men's breeches and a dusty tunic." Lord Langtry smiled. "Mayhap you should keep the lady for your own. I'm sorry, my lord, that it took so long for us to come and get you. We had a devil of a time locating you."

The lady would be way too much of a handful. And Duke Tully could not see keeping her confined when he was sure she wouldn't be a willing bride. Her mother would hunt him down on top of that. As well as would her brother and cousins. It was best to ransom her for the money it could bring. His king would enjoy his share and be amused to boot. "You are certain they did not find a way out already?"

"Nay, we are not certain of that, my lord. If they found another exit, we know not where it is."

Lord Langtry preceded the duke into the tunnels. Duke Tully followed and his five other men after that, while one remained behind as lookout.

After traversing the tunnels for what seemed an eternity, they came upon an arrow carved into a rock facing. "Newly marked," Lord Langtry whispered. "They've come this way."

Duke Tully smiled, already anticipating how much money this could mean to him, but capturing the dark fae princess was an added bonus.

STARTLED AWAKE by the sound of men's boots tromping down one of the tunnels, Ritasia sat up and tugged at King Tiernan's tunic. "Someone's coming," she whispered. "Sounds like several men."

Why was she whispering, when it probably was some of her own people? Because no one was calling out her name. And that made her fear that whoever it was were thieves.

King Tiernan pulled her to her feet, but she felt cold and stiff and achy. Even though he'd helped to warm her by keeping her off the floor and kept his arms wrapped tight around her, it hadn't kept all the chill out of her bones. And she was hungry. Sitting beside the king at the evening meal, she'd been so conscious of the way he was sitting so close to her, whispering into her ear, making her people believe he was ready to snatch her up and marry her, that she'd barely been able to eat.

The fae didn't need to eat. Not really. But they did so as a form of celebration and they did get hungry when they didn't partake in regular meals. She supposed it was kind of like when a human had finished a meal but was still craving having something else to eat— like a hot fudge sundae even though he didn't really need it to slake a hunger.

"Come." King Tiernan moved her away from the sound of the boots tromping through the tunnel but quickly pulled her to a halt when the footfalls stopped abruptly. Both her breath and the king's were puffs of mist in the chilly air. "They are trying to determine where we are by the sound of our footfalls."

"We cannot take off our boots," she said in a hushed voice back. "The ground's too rocky."

"Not here," he said, sliding his foot across the path. "It's still smooth here."

"This had to be a main path closer to the castle," she said, thinking surely it was, though how that would help them, she didn't know when the castle above was no more.

"We might find another trapdoor." He let go of her hand and crouched in front of her.

"What are you doing?" she asked, her heart racing.

His hands were on her calves as he reached to touch her knee-high boots. "We must remove our boots. It won't give us a lot of time unless they take the wrong path that moves them away from us. But at least they won't be able to hear us."

"They are not my men, are they?"

"They would have called out for you," he said, saying just what she'd been thinking.

Then he had their boots under his arm and her hand in his as they silently moved forward.

"Do you think they found your arrow carvings?"

"Aye," he whispered against her temple.

"They are the bad guys."

But he didn't agree or disagree. Still, she knew he thought the same as she did, or they would not be trying to avoid the men.

They were not the good guys.

KING TIERNAN HAD FOUGHT in many battles, protecting his people from the closest major kingdom there was, that of the griffon fae of the island realm, and he'd found himself avoiding capture on four different occasions when he and his men had become separated. So he was used to such maneuvers and was quite successful at it.

Except for one thing. He'd never had a princess, or any other woman for that matter, under his care that he had to protect at the same time. And back home, he was familiar with his lands and that of the island kingdom, not like here.

Of all the times that he'd been faced with the dilemma of being stalked by his enemy, this was one time that he decidedly did not want to fall into the enemy's hands.

"If the men are not common thieves," he asked Ritasia, "who else might they be?" It was important to know who their enemy was.

"Duke Tully and his men who often take high-ranked officials hostage for a ransom."

"A duke?" said in surprise. "He works alone?"

"He is a dragon fae, and it is said his king receives a payment from Duke Tully's reward."

"Dragon fae," King Tiernan growled. If he heard one more thing about the troublesome dragon fae…

"There," Ritasia whispered, tugging him to a set of stairs, hoping it was a way out. "I see a scant bit of light through there. Do you see it?"

"It's a different set of stairs." But King Tiernan didn't sound as enthusiastic as she did.

"Aye. It has to be a way out."

He climbed to the top of the stairs and pressed against the trapdoor. When it didn't immediately open, he thrust up with his back and the door creaked.

Ritasia's heart nearly gave out as she knew the men who had been following them would have heard the creaking noise echo through the tunnels.

"What is it?" she asked, waiting for him to climb through the opening.

"A cellar. Wine cellar," he said, offering his hand and then pulling her through the opening. He quickly lowered the trapdoor, which had the nerve to creak again.

She used her fae light to illuminate the small underground room filled with racks of dusty wine-filled bottles. The crazy notion came to her that the wine was so aged it probably was priceless. Though what good that knowledge did her, she didn't know.

A rumbling sound behind her made her jump and whip around, expecting to see an army of men fill the cellar. But Tiernan was shoving a rack of wine over the trapdoor.

"We're trapped," she said.

"No. The archaeologists will find the tunnels. They will put out word about the men combing them, searching for us. Someone from your kingdom will find us."

The sound of running boots caught their attention and both

Tiernan and Ritasia stared at the trapdoor, hoping it would hold. A thud sounded against it. Then several more.

"They are up there, my lord. They have barricaded themselves in. But they cannot get out. At least we do not think they can."

"Her people will be searching for her. If they discover the trapdoor into the tunnels, they will be down here in droves, Lord Tully."

Someone paced back and forth down below. Then one of the men said, "We will have to leave. Some other time, my sweet," he called out as if speaking to Ritasia.

"Duke Tully," Ritasia whispered. At least she guessed that it was him speaking.

The boots clomped on the stone floor away from the trapdoor.

Neither Tiernan nor Ritasia said a word. Then finally she whispered to him, "Do you think they have left?"

"Mayhap." Tiernan began to inspect the room. "'Tis also possible a man or two lies in wait in case we leave..." He broke off abruptly.

"What?" she asked, looking up from the trapdoor where she had been listening for any sound that might indicate a man had been left behind.

"Another narrow stairs. These most likely led into the kitchen. The other was the escape route into the tunnels."

Ritasia hurried to join him, hope returning that they might find a way out yet. Once they pushed open the trapdoor and were able to leave the room, they could fae transport back to the castle.

Where her mother would kill her.

Ritasia watched as Tiernan tried to lift the door. It would give only a slight bit and then would open no further. "What is blocking it?"

"A fallen pillar, I believe," Tiernan said.

But she wouldn't let it make her lose hope. If there was one rule she strictly adhered to in life was that she never gave up. "Hold the door as far as it will go, and I will squirm through."

"What if our enemy is waiting up there?"

"I will fae transport and return with soldiers to rescue you."

She could tell from his expression that he did not like the notion. But it was the only solution she could think of.

"We should wait here," he said.

"Nay. We must take the advantage. If Duke Tully's men are in the tunnels, my mother's guard could capture them."

"I don't like it."

"We cannot stay down here forever." Then she frowned at him, remembering—despite how commanding he was as if he was in charge—that he wasn't. Not of her, in any case. "These are my lands, my kingdom, and you have no say in what I do."

That brought an evil smile to his lips. But before he let go of the trapdoor and kept her from doing what she planned to do next, she began to climb through. He couldn't very well let the trapdoor squish her. Even if he wanted to keep her with him by any means.

Cursing, he held it up for her while she wriggled and squirmed and was afraid she might get stuck. But then she finally managed to wiggle the rest of the way through, and when she fell onto the floor, she took a deep breath and flashed her fae light about.

"What do you see?" Tiernan demanded, angry with her, and she imagined angry with himself for not being able to stop her or follow her.

"A very ancient kitchen it appears. Fireplaces, iron cauldrons, wooden beams high above, cracks in the walls where some light is coming through. No windows though."

"Is there a way out?" he called to her, sounding both exasperated and worried.

"I...do not know. Wait. I see a small door."

"Ritasia, wait."

"I will be right back."

"I have got your dagger," he said, sounding more than concerned for her.

He had her boots, too, she belatedly realized. But while he held up the trapdoor, he couldn't have slipped either her dagger or boots to her.

"I will be all right," she assured him.

She crossed the short distance to the door, and when she carefully opened it, the hinges creaked in protest, giving her heart a jump. If anyone was in the vicinity, they would know she was here.

Taking a deep breath, she peered into the room and found a great hall, no sign of any inhabitants for centuries, except for a trail of little prints in the dust coating the floor—rats, she thought and gave a little shudder.

She stared at the place in awe, though. Ancient fae had once dined at the long trestle tables and wooden benches as her people now dined in their castle's great hall. But there were no tapestries on the walls, only sconces for torches long since extinguished, the black scorches from the flames evident on the stone walls, and cobwebs hanging in corners like great spun silky decorations, also coated in dust. No tapestries on the cold floor either. Just thick layers of dust.

She hurried through the room and found a winding staircase blocked by debris. She squirmed her way through the dirt and timber and over a fallen pillar until she found a passageway to doors leading to a number of bedchambers, she assumed, if it was anything like her castle.

She opened the first door and stared at the room that looked as though it had been preserved for the fae queen herself for all time. A small light streamed through an arrow slotted window. When she looked around, she saw three more for defending the castle, but no window bigger than that, and no way could she fit through one. She hurried to the closest one and peered out, wondering why they couldn't have seen the tower from the dig site.

She realized then that the tower was built into the rocky cliffs. The rest would have towered above this and shown up above where now stood broken pillars. No one could venture close to the cliffs because of the coral reef barriers that prevented ships getting near the treacherous rocky shore.

She turned and glanced around the room. Everything was coated in a thick layer of dust, of course, but even so, she could see how regal the furniture was, every piece intricately carved hard woods, and opulently decorated mosaics painted on the walls and ceilings, the muted golds and silvers revealing that no expense had been spared.

The bed curtains and linens were the richest velvet fabrics of forest green, and all the material was embellished with golden flowers and leaves.

She wondered again where all the people had vanished to. What tragedy had befallen them?

An overwhelming sense of sorrow shook her to the core. She didn't think that seeing something like this would mean anything to anyone but those who were fascinated with the past. But that was because she'd never viewed an entire room that looked just like hers, except tons dustier and decorated differently. It wasn't just a bone left buried under rubble, or a half rotted golden slipper, but a place where someone had actually lived.

Chill bumps erupted over her arms as she stared at the closed curtains over the bed. Would someone still be in there? Long ago dead?

Barely breathing, she moved toward the bed, her heart thundering. She couldn't shake loose of the fear, despite knowing nothing could hurt her. Not someone who had been dead for centuries. But she was afraid to look, not wanting to see a corpse and remember the queen that way forever. Yet she couldn't avoid looking either.

She had to know. Was the queen in the bed?

Her hand shaking, Ritasia reached for the curtain, gripped it, fortified herself, and slid it slowly aside, the wooden rings lightly scraping as they slid across the wooden pole.

The bed was empty. The bedcovers had been pulled back as if the queen's maid had prepared it for her, waiting for her mistress to return to bed. But there was no one there. Just once fresh red rose petals and purple lavender now wizened and muted in color. And a strand of dark hair on a lumpy pillow resting at the headboard. It reminded her of the comb and the dark hair.

She took in a deep breath to steady her nerves, relieved that she hadn't found an emaciated body in the bed.

"Ritasia!" King Tiernan shouted, sounding a million miles away. Yet his voice made her jump.

"I am all right!" she yelled back, hoping that her voice would carry that far.

She turned and studied the table, a gold hand mirror lying on top, lace doilies, a jeweled brass goblet and a silver tray, both badly tarnished. She crossed the floor to the table and peered into the goblet, expecting to see it filled with wine or ale, but if it had been, any remnants were long gone and now it was only filled with dust.

The comb she had in her pouch was the kind decorated in jewels that a lady wore to keep her hair secured. Ritasia looked again at the mirror and decided then that the comb belonged here with the ghosts of the past. Not tucked away in some vault of the dark fae kingdom. It belonged here with the ancient fae that once had flourished in all its glory.

But then a glint of something silver caught her eye, the object half-buried under one of the lady's lacy doilies, distracting her. She lifted the dusty, once pale blue fabric. A medallion she had never seen before lay on the table, a snake curling around a scepter engraved on it. Her mouth dropped a little. This was a fae that none of their people knew existed. Their scholars would want to know that another fae had lived here once. Is this what her mother had been searching for? To discover who the ancient fae really had been?

And yet, she thought...a silver medallion meant it belonged to the unseelie fae.

So that she wouldn't lose it, Ritasia pulled the chain over her head, then caught sight of a golden box. She moved closer and lifted the lid. Inside were dozens of jeweled rings, bracelets, necklaces, and hair ornaments.

Unlike all the rest of the jewelry, one small ring stood out, its simple design of a Celtic knot catching her attention. Something about its simplicity made her wonder what significance it had to have been sitting with all the other jewelry that was truly dazzling, when this one was not.

King Tiernan yelled again for her.

"I am okay!" she shouted again, glanced down at the ring in the palm of her hand and meant to put it back in the box, but couldn't. What was there about the ring that seemed so...intriguing? It felt almost...warm to the touch, as if it belonged to her. Which was bizarre. She would take it back and show it to Malathon and ask him why this plain silver ring would have been placed with jewelry that had to have been worth a fortune.

So as not to lose it, she slipped it onto her finger, then hurried out of the queen's chambers and headed down the hall. Surely there had to be a way out of this castle other than through the tunnels and that one trapdoor. One of the rooms had to have a window...

Wait. She stopped abruptly. She was above the iron ore rock walls of the tunnels. She should be able to fae transport, although she was afraid she wouldn't know how to find the cellar again.

Hating to leave Tiernan behind, she knew she had to get help. With that thought in mind, she attempted to fae travel. Nothing happened. She just stood there. Going nowhere. She tried again. Again, no luck and this time she swore under her breath.

She stared at the walls, then ran her fingers over the roughly hewn stone. Were they filled with iron ore also? No one in the castle could have fae transported to the outside then. But then again, no one could have breached their defenses with fae travel either.

She hurried to the next door, figuring one of the walls might have collapsed to one of the rooms, and she could get out that way. But when she pulled the door open, she heard the most awful grinding sound.

And felt the floor beneath her feet give way just before she screamed.

HEART DRUMMING WITH FEAR, King Tiernan heard the racket from far away right before Ritasia screamed.

Something had collapsed.

"Ritasia!" he yelled. He envisioned the whole ceiling above her had fallen in, and she was buried alive. "Ritasia!"

He shoved at the trapdoor above him, but he couldn't budge the pillar blocking it, nor could he crawl through the narrow opening like the princess had done. She had barely been able to herself.

"Ritasia!"

He hoped to the goddess, she would return and assure him she was all right. But no matter how much he prayed it was so, or called out her name, she made no answering call back.

He cursed to high heaven and then when he was through with dealing with the self-recriminations, he acted. If any of the men in the tunnels thought to take him hostage, they'd best think again. He ran down the narrow steps, stalked through the cellar where he found his boots and slipped them on, and tucked Ritasia's under his belt. Then he shoved the wine rack out of the way and threw the trapdoor to the tunnels aside. If anyone was waiting for him, he did not see them.

He hurried down the stairs and quickly moved into the tunnel, intending to locate the area where he thought the ceiling above Ritasia or the floor beneath her must have caved in. Just around the bend, two men waited for him, arrows nocked and ready to shoot. Both were dressed in green tunics and leggings, their boots brown, their hair blond and disheveled from the wind. Both eyed him with speculation, measuring him for his fighting potential.

"Something has collapsed somewhere in that direction, and I fear that Princess Ritasia may have been injured," Tiernan said scowling, jerking his hand toward the south. Not that he knew that was what had happened. It very well could be that a floor above her had collapsed and buried her, or that the one she had been standing on had given way. Or just a wall had fallen over. Or that she was knocked unconscious and not buried at all. Any scenario he could come up with gave him heart palpitations.

"Either you help me to locate and save her, or I kill you. *Both.*"

Tiernan took a menacing step forward, and the men's smiles faded. "Who are we addressing?" the taller of the two said. They did not look intimidated, but Tiernan wasn't backing down.

"King Tiernan of the hawk fae. Niceties aside, the lady could be in grave danger."

Neither man lowered his bow.

"Fine," he said and charged toward them with murder in his eyes, Ritasia's dagger gripped fiercely in his hand before he even realized he'd drawn it out.

"Wait," the one said, still standing his ground. "I'm Lord Larkin and this Sir Olaf. Show us where the princess can be found."

"We cannot go that way," Tiernan said, motioning to the stairs to the cellar. "A pillar blocks the trapdoor that leads into the kitchen."

"Maybe with the three of us shoving at it—," Lord Larkin said.

"No, the space on the stairs has only enough room for one man to stand at a time."

Lord Larkin looked speculatively at Tiernan. "If we rescue the princess, what will we get out of the deal?"

"You shall live," Tiernan snarled, and shoved past the men. He had no time for mercenaries or thieves.

Lord Larkin and the knight chuckled. But Tiernan was serious.

"Where are you going?" Lord Larkin asked.

"In the direction I heard something give out." Tiernan glanced back at Lord Larkin. "Do you work for Duke Tully?"

"Aye."

"Dragon fae," Tiernan sneered. "If you do not help me..."

"I know. We shall die." Lord Larkin sounded more amused at the notion than worried, and Tiernan assumed he might have to make his point clearer at some point before long.

Footfalls behind the two men made them all turn to see who had arrived now.

Four more men headed for them, all wearing forest green clothes, no doubt to blend in with their surroundings before they pounced on unsuspecting prey.

"Where is the princess?" one of the men asked in a brusque and annoyed toned.

Tiernan suspected the man was Duke Tully. He had a jovial look about him, not at all like what Tiernan would have depicted for a nobleman who took highly ranked fae hostage. He had expected someone harder, more cynical, and more sinister.

The duke was tall like Tiernan, his gray-blue eyes assessing his opponent.

"She may have been injured somewhere in this direction," Lord Larkin said. "This is King Tiernan, of the hawk fae kingdom."

The duke's expression subtly changed. Was he trying to determine if Tiernan sat on a throne but never fought in any battle, like some kings were known to do? Truth be known, all the hawk fae heirs to the throne were well trained in battle while in exile. At least until they took the throne. Or maybe Duke Tully felt a little out of his league because he knew little about the hawk fae? Or that he was addressing a king of a major kingdom?

Though the duke appeared a congenial sort, he was still a mercenary at heart and was not to be trusted.

"My...my, and you have been alone with the lady all night long?" the duke asked, his tone more of a warning now. The dragon fae might not be allies with the lion fae, but all of a sudden a hawk fae from around the world steps in and might have compromised one of the noblewomen living in this hemisphere? "Queen Irenis will not like it."

"The queen will not like that you had intended to take the lady hostage," Tiernan growled, throwing the truth back at the duke.

No one said anything for a while as the sound of boots pounded on rock.

Duke Tully finally said, "When we find the lady—"

"King Tiernan," Lord Larkin said, good naturedly, "will allow us to go on our way without any harm done."

"He says this, does he?" The duke's tone of voice was ripe with humor.

"Which member of the dragon fae court had Princess Ritasia locked in the dungeon?" Tiernan asked, glowering over his shoulder at Duke Tully.

"Not any of us." And for the first time since the amiable nobleman had spoken to him, Tiernan noted the disapproval and the wariness in the lord's voice.

He must have finally suspected that where the lady was concerned, Tiernan would allow no quarter.

Again, silence filled the air as Tiernan listened for any sounds that might indicate Ritasia was nearby.

Duke Tully finally cleared his throat. "Do you intend to marry the lady?"

Tiernan scowled at him. "'Tis none of your concern."

The duke stiffened. "You are not of this region, yet you take a lady, a princess, no less, into an unsafe place and are with her unchaperoned for hours and you say it does not concern me?"

"You were going to take her hostage!" Tiernan roared.

No one said anything to that and Tiernan realized no matter that Duke Tully was a common thief, he was also noble by birth and seemed to stand by noble ways—as far as they suited him.

Duke Tully said, "I would have found a lady to accompany her until her mother paid up. I would not have compromised her."

Tiernan snorted. Then he thought he heard some sound to their left and turned into another tunnel. This time, he found a door at the end of the tunnel. Expecting the door to be blocked or bolted, he shoved as hard as he could. The door was wedged against fallen timbers and left only a narrow passage to be traversed.

"Ritasia?" he called out. He squeezed between the door and the frame and scrambled over the debris in the cavernous room, devoid of all but half-demolished packing crates and ceiling joists and flooring from above that had fallen to the floor. He heard a moan off to his right in the dark and waved his fae light in that direction. "Ritasia!"

He couldn't see her and could barely breathe from all the dust stirred up by the collapsed ceiling, particles floating in the air like tiny fairies on wing.

Before he could head in the direction he'd heard her moan, Duke Tully grabbed his arm and stopped him. Tiernan gave him a killing look, but the duke motioned to the ceiling. "More of it is ready to collapse, my lord."

Tiernan glanced up and saw that the duke was right, that several timbers that had been holding the upper floor were leaning deep into the cavern and any slight movement could send them tumbling to the rocky floor.

Getting his temper under control, Tiernan nodded and moved to the perimeter. "Ritasia," Tiernan hollered, seeking any response.

She moaned again.

His heart nearly gave out. He skirted around the edge of the collapse, climbing over debris until he saw her. She was half buried in timbers and dirt, her nearly black hair red with dust, her ivory skin paler, her face pinched in pain. He scrambled over two fallen timbers and other remnants of the floor that would have been above their heads only minutes ago to get to her. Two of the other men were close on his heels.

"Ritasia," he said, pulling away the timbers as the other men helped to ease them away from her. "Are you hurt?" He knew she had to be from the look on her face. She was so pale, her face grimacing in pain as they moved every piece of wood off her.

"I broke my arm, I believe." She sounded like she was annoyed with herself, and he almost smiled.

She was in pain, had to be bruised, maybe injured elsewhere other than her arm, but instead of being weak and acquiescent, she was highly pissed.

He and Duke Tully removed the rest of the debris from her as carefully as they could. Then Tiernan drew her from the remaining flooring, careful with her arm as she held it close to her body, gritting her teeth as he lifted her from the floor.

"Come," Duke Tully said. "We will lead you to the surface."

Tiernan carried her in his arms, trying not to jar her too much. He felt the tension in her body, heard the moans she attempted to conceal, and knew she was fighting valiantly not to reveal how much she was hurting. He suspected she was annoyed that they had to resort to dealing with Duke Tully and his men in the end.

Then they took off down the tunnel and walked and walked and walked some more. The way seemed to take forever, but when they reached the surface, Tiernan expected to see the digs. Instead, this trapdoor opened onto a rocky ledge with no way to go but to fae transport. No living soul except a bird or two could have made their way to and off this ledge as it looked out to the misty laden sea.

"He said he would actually kill us if we did not help him with finding and rescuing the princess," Lord Larkin said with a grin.

"Did he now?" Duke Tully said with a return smile.

Their tone of voices warned Tiernan they were up to no good.

He called on his ability to transport Ritasia and himself back to the dark fae castle, when Sir Olaf clamped his leg with a fae iron.

7

"The dragon fae are not to be trusted at any cost," Tiernan growled, sitting on a brown wool blanket in front of a blazing fire crackling and popping, the flames lighting the area near it in an orange glow. The smell of wood smoke mixed with the crisp, cold breeze.

He glowered at Duke Tully, watching him from across the flickering orange-red flames, two other guards posted nearby.

Furious with himself, Tiernan should have known better. But he had been so relieved to take the princess out of the tunnels and so startled to see the cliffs and not the dig site when they climbed out, he hadn't reacted quickly enough.

As if they were free-spirited wood nymphs, women dressed in forest green gowns, their long hair loose and wild cascading over their shoulders, danced to lilting flute music and the strum of a banjo around another campfire nearby. A couple of men spitted a wild boar over another fire some distance from the one Tiernan sat beside. Green canvas tents were scattered through the forest, and he wondered just how long Tully and his men...and women had lived here. Or was it just a temporary camp? He couldn't imagine anyone ransoming the wealthy for money, then living in the woods without being able to enjoy the finer amenities of life, food, housing, and clothes that one could well afford.

He studied Ritasia, her skin milk-white, her coal black lashes fanning her cheeks, her long dark hair in curls—none of it bound any longer—framing her delicate face. Her broken arm was bound in green cloth as she slept on a mat some distance away, an olive-green wool blanket tucked under her arms, a pillow beneath her head. She was sleeping soundly, and he presumed they had given her some kind of sedative to ease the pain.

Duke Tully motioned to Ritasia. "She would not leave you behind, though I gave her every opportunity to do so. She was free to go home. I would not keep the injured princess against her will."

Tiernan continued to consider Ritasia, not sparing Tully a glance. The princess appeared to be comfortable. He couldn't imagine why she wouldn't have returned home, given the opportunity. She might have been able to send an army to free him. Or maybe not. Maybe she didn't have any clue as to where they were any more than he did. Or maybe Tully hadn't given her the opportunity, as he said he had. The man was not to be trusted. He was a dragon fae, for one. And his occupation wasn't honorable.

Tully poked a stick in the fire. "I am not the enemy."

At that comment, Tiernan sliced him a glare.

A hint of a smile brightened Tully's naturally jovial face. "I have given you the perfect alibi. Instead of you being alone in the tunnels all night with the lady, you were my guests. As you can see," he said, motioning to the ladies dancing so cheerily, silhouetted by the bright flames and dark night, "we have many lovely ladies in attendance who will attest to your good behavior concerning the princess."

"You are still seeking a ransom?" Tiernan did not believe the man was that magnanimous.

"In due time," the duke said. "One of my men said that Prince Deveron and his cousins Micala and Niall and a dozen trackers have found your fae dust trails in the tunnels. They have also found mine. They will know it hasn't been long since we took you both hostage. But we have returned to the forests of our dragon fae kingdom. The queen can either send her men into the forests and hope to catch me but in so doing so alienate my king and threaten war, or she can besiege my king to order me to release you both into the queen's care."

"And?" Tiernan asked, not understanding the strange politics in this region.

"Well, that's the mystery now, isn't it? We have no way of knowing which way it will go. 'Tis possible Queen Irenis will ask the king to order me to free you both while her son takes men to search for me in the interim."

"I should have killed you all when I had the chance."

Duke Tully smiled. "I have heard it rumored that the hawk fae kings are tyrants. Does the lady know this? Or is this just a myth created by parents who wish their little ones to fear the might of such a king?"

"It is true, and you should be conscious of that fact for your own health." Tiernan rose from his seated position and folded his arms. "Send her back," he growled.

Duke Tully chuckled. "Against her wishes? A tyrant who seeks the lady's hand would not wish to be parted from her. I do not believe you are as much a despot as you wish me to believe."

RITASIA LISTENED to Duke Tully as he spoke to King Tiernan, while she pretended to sleep on the bedding. Although she *was* half asleep, unable to shake off the lethargy she was feeling. What he said was true about her not wishing to return home alone without King Tiernan. She had no idea where they were, and she'd never be able to bring troops back here to free him. Though she didn't remember Duke Tully giving her a choice. He might have. But she just couldn't remember.

If she could get close enough to Tiernan, she could transport them both out of here, even though he was wearing the fae manacles.

But when Duke Tully said the hawk fae king was known to be a tyrant, that had given her pause. Was he? Around her own people, he seemed gracious, but among his men was he the devil?

He certainly didn't seem that way, but then again, he was considering her as a bride choice and was probably on his best behavior.

Was that why he had to leave his homeland in search of a bride?

She considered her surroundings and the joy that filled the air —the laughter and singing, the jokes and good-hearted cama- raderie. The aroma of the pork, wood smoke, pine needles, and crisp cold freshness scented the air. If she and the king were not prisoners, she would have enjoyed the festivities.

Now she understood why Duke Tully and his men were called the band of merry hostage takers. Everyone seemed of good spirits. Except for Tiernan. She imagined he was the kind of warrior that did not take being captured by the enemy—any enemy—well.

She didn't like it either, though. She had to admit her curiosity concerning the duke was satisfied, and she never wanted to make his acquaintance again. The king was probably also feeling remiss in keeping her out of the grasp of these men's hands. But he wasn't at fault.

Tiernan scowled at Duke Tully who appeared perfectly pleased with himself.

She thought of her mother and what she would want. She would wish Ritasia left the king behind and returned home at once. Or would she? If her mother wished to make an alliance with the hawk fae kingdom, she might not want Ritasia to leave the king at all.

If only everyone would go to sleep, then Ritasia would slip near him and grab his arm, and they would be off! She was pretty sure she wasn't wearing a fae shackle. A blanket covered her, but she didn't feel a manacle around either of her ankles.

Someone had given her a healing draught and between that and her fae healing abilities, her arm was on the mend already. Although it would still take a couple of days before the bone was fully healed. But at least the pain had subsided a good deal. And she was lucky it was her left arm and not her right. Yet she felt...not quite herself, as if she wasn't all here, exactly.

She drifted off but woke when it grew completely quiet in the camp, no more music or dancing, no more conversations, just the breeze ruffling the tree branches and the crackling of the campfires.

Ritasia chanced a glance in Tiernan's direction again. He was studying her. She didn't know if he could see her very well in the dark as far away as she was from him. He was still sitting beside the red-flamed fire, and she could see his anxious expression. And then, his eyes widened a bit, and she believed he could see she was looking at him.

She glanced over at the fire to see who else was sitting around it. Duke Tully was nowhere in sight. But two of his men were watching the fire and Tiernan still.

"Want some more ale?" the one guard said to the other, taking his eyes off the fire and Tiernan for a minute.

"Aye. I'll watch the prisoner."

One guard would always be posted, Ritasia thought. She didn't believe she would have a better chance at rescuing Tiernan and herself with only one, instead of two guards posted. She sat up but felt her world spinning and closed her eyes. What had they given her?

No matter. She had to attempt this now. She concentrated on Tiernan, his eyes widening even further, but he quickly looked back at the guard, and she did too. The guard grabbed another log for the fire and tossed it on top, sending orange sparks flying through the dark night and a barrage of fresh crackling noises erupted.

Ritasia meant to transport next to the king, grab his arm, and take him away. Instead, she vanished and reappeared in the woods some distance from the camp, realizing at once the king still had her boots. She heard low voices somewhere in the camp from here, saw the campfires glowing through the woods, knew she wasn't too far away from where Tiernan sat. But if anyone noticed she'd vanished...

Cursing herself for her inability to control her movement, she hoped Tiernan didn't believe she'd left him behind and went home.

But maybe that was a good thing. Maybe, if the guard noticed she'd left, they would think no one could rescue Tiernan, and they wouldn't be on guard so much. She took a deep breath, still couldn't get her dizziness under control, and tried to transport near the fire again, hoping she didn't land in it, the way her mind seemed so unwilling to focus.

She appeared next to a dark green tent, glad she hadn't landed on top of it and squished the sleeping occupant. A black dragon flag waved proudly in the cool breeze beside it, and she figured it was Duke Tully's tent, since no flags flew near other tents in the vicinity.

Great.

She would try once more, and if that didn't work, she was just walking over to where King Tiernan sat beside the fire, wherever it was from the duke's tent. Even though she was certain her stocking feet would protest. She would run, but she felt so dizzy, she didn't think she would get very far before she stumbled over her own feet. Walking seemed a safer mode of transportation.

If she could just grab Tiernan's arm, she could transport him to the woods nearby, or somewhere else. Just anywhere. And she could keep transporting them until she was far enough away to make their escape. Maybe.

At least she wasn't giving up trying.

Footfalls headed in her direction, nearly giving her a seizure. Someone stalked toward Duke Tully's tent at a fast pace, and she crouched down behind it, nearly falling she felt so out of it, so discombobulated.

She could see a smidgeon of the guard in the dark. He was tall, fierce, and his expression angry. He was the guard who'd left the campfire to fetch ale, leaving the other alone to watch King Tiernan. "My lord," the man said, his voice urgent, concerned, as he stood next to the opening of the duke's tent. "The princess has vanished."

Her heart flipped over. They knew. And now Duke Tully would be warned while she crouched next to his tent in the dark shadows.

Duke Tully didn't answer.

"My lord," the man said a little louder this time.

"What?" Duke Tully asked, sounding tired and grouchy.

"Princess Ritasia, my lord. She has vanished."

Movement inside the tent followed, and then the duke walked out of his tent, wearing only his breeches. "What? The drug should have kept her asleep."

They had drugged her. Well, they might have intended for it to keep her asleep. But she was very much awake. Kind of.

"Let me get dressed. Wake the healer. I want to know what effect the drug will have on her transporting herself somewhere else. If she's close by, we need to find her at once."

"And?"

Duke Tully gave a derisive snort. "Lock her in fae iron."

"Aye, my lord."

So much for the duke's comment that he had allowed her to leave of her own free will. Instead, he'd figured the drug had kept her from going anywhere.

Duke Tully whipped around and reentered his tent as the guard stalked off to another part of camp. Ritasia concentrated the best she could and transported again. She wasn't sure if she was so dizzy and disoriented from the rapid transporting, even though she was not going far, or if it was the drug, or a combination of both, but she thought she was sitting in the king's lap.

He smiled down at her and whispered, "Did you wish to take me somewhere, my fae princess?"

A guard rushed around the fire to reach them, and she meant to grab the king's arm, but he had his arms wrapped soundly around her in a warm embrace, and she thought about how much she wanted to get far away from here—which was the way to transport, only she needed a destination, and she couldn't think of one. Not with the shouting from the guard and several others as the camp woke in a rush.

"She's here!" the guard shouted, trying to reach the king and her.

She was confused, but she knew she had to make the right decision. To take him far away from here. And she considered so many places they could go that she thought would be safe for them—the Renaissance fairgrounds at Waxahachie that were closed for the season, even if it was dragon fae-claimed territory, South Padre Island, the dark fae territory, her own bedchambers, even the minor turtle fae kingdom where some of her cousins resided.

She thought of a beach and the night and no people, no shouting, no rallying of the troops, right before she remembered her mother had forbidden her to go to South Padre Island, and then the world shifted.

Tiernan still had his arms securely wrapped around Ritasia, still seated as before, only they were no longer at the campfire in the woods but sitting upon a beach. He wondered where in the world she'd brought them. The human plane of existence? In their own world somewhere near the Denkar fae castle? He didn't know the land well enough to recognize the place. But he was glad she was so resourceful, although he could tell she was quite dazed from whatever drug they'd given her.

The night was still dark as they sat on the sandy beach, ocean waves crashing on the shore some distance hence, a soft warm breeze blowing over them, the smell of salt and fish and seaweed. But Ritasia was sound asleep in his arms as he sat on the warm sand.

He could see the minx would need his firm hand in ensuring she remained safe. She seemed to be the kind of woman who enjoyed living life in a more...adventurous way. Very much like himself. Only when it came to him, he could get away with it, being a man and a king, after all.

He couldn't see her being the perfect courtly queen, dressed in all her finery, surrounded by her maids, participating only in those activities that seemed suitable for a fae queen to take part in. Even now she was still dressed in her dusty male breeches and tunic and boots, and he just couldn't envision her wearing anything else.

He should have known what she was truly like once he'd seen her scrambling over fallen pillars at the dig site, and when Prince Raglan had told him she had ended up in a dragon fae dungeon. Which he still intended to learn more about.

And the fact that her brother and cousins could dare her to take part in some risky adventure, and she would go along with it also. Not only that, but she had appeared at the court dressed in the tunic, dusty male breeches, and that floppy adventurer's hat that had half hidden her beauty, then she had told him to sit in her cousin's seat. Oh, aye, she was not the queen he had ever dreamed would be his own.

He smiled and tightened his hold on her. She seemed perfect

for the role as his queen. Perfect for a tyrant king descended from a long line of tyrant kings.

He looked down at her, her sweet face cloaked in sleep under the light of the full moon. At this very instant, she appeared charming, angelic, and he had to smile at the notion. She was anything but. Although he had to admit he greatly admired her for staying with him at Duke Tully's camp, while making every effort to help him escape, despite her condition.

At first, he had assumed she'd woken enough to decide to try and help him, though she had looked dazed. Then when she disappeared and did not reappear next to him, he figured she'd gone home and had planned to get help. He couldn't believe it when she miscalculated her transport and ended up in his lap, intending to rescue him all on her own. She was a treasure.

He sighed. They needed to return to her people and assure them she was all right. If only he could transport them, he would, but he had no way of removing the manacle around his ankle.

Then he noted the two chains she wore around her neck. The lion fae medallion, most likely. But what was the other? He hadn't noticed it before this.

With his free hand, he reached down to pull at the chains and slip them out of her tunic so that he could examine them. The lion-embossed golden medallion was on top. A silver medallion was eclipsed by the other. He slid the lion fae medallion aside and saw the engraving of a snake coiled around a scepter, the snake's fangs exposed, ready to strike its prey.

He stared at the familiar sign that he'd seen in ancient journals depicting the ancient fae kingdoms, both of seelie and unseelie courts. This one was the symbol of the unseelie fae. He glanced up at Ritasia. Why would she have a medallion of an unseelie fae court and why was she wearing it?

He had no sooner wondered about the medallion when he heard movement in the sand behind him. Six men rushed across the sand dressed in red uniforms trimmed in silver braid, guards of some fae kingdom. But not Ritasia's kingdom.

That's when he saw the silver rings around their eyes glowing brightly, the fierce scowls they wore, the determination in their stride, and the swords withdrawn. King Tiernan swore under his breath. How in the hell had they ended up in the unseelie fae plane?

"Seelie," one of the men snarled in anger. "What are you doing *here*?"

"Ritasia," he whispered to her, not wishing to alarm her, but he had to wake her and have her quickly transport them out of here.

Her eyes fluttered open, and she glanced up with a sleepy kind of look, her long black lashes nearly hiding her half-shuttered eyes. "Tiernan?" she said softly.

"Aye, you have brought us to the unseelie plane. Take us out of here at once," he ordered, trying to break through the impenetrable fog she seemed to be in.

"He has no power," the one guard said. "Kill him. But the girl, we will bring her before the king, and he will decide what he will do with her."

Ritasia's gaze shifted to the unseelie who was speaking. She whispered to Tiernan. "Oh, my goddess, how did we get here?"

"You brought us. Take us away."

She closed her eyes and he feared she would fall asleep again, but they were suddenly enveloped in thick mist. The footfalls of the guards on the beach abruptly stopped.

"What...what has she done? Where are they?" one of the men said.

Tiernan wasn't sure what Ritasia had done, but they were still close to where the guards were, and no mist would deter them.

And then he and Ritasia were no longer sitting on the beach but sitting on a bare stone floor in a castle's great hall, not any that

Tiernan had been in before, the walls covered with tapestries depicting fae fighting with fae of other kingdoms.

The scent of the fae who lived here was the same as the scent from those on the beach. "Unseelie kingdom," Tiernan warned Ritasia, before they were discovered once again. "How are you taking us through the unseelie plane?"

No one was in the place, thank the goddess. Everyone but the guards on duty must still be in bed at this early hour. But it didn't mean someone might not come along and run across them.

Only in the ancient past had the unseelie and seelie courts found a way to rip apart the fabric that kept those from one plane from visiting those of another. After much killing, it was said a truce between the planes healed the fabric, and never again could the two courts meet. Except when in the human world. But even then, they avoided each other as if any interaction would seal their doom.

"I don't know how I did this," she whispered, sounding worried and perplexed.

He glanced down at the medallion she now wore. "Where did you get that?" He studied the snake coiled around the scepter on the medallion. "It's an ancient unseelie fae symbol."

She raised the ring to examine it, and he noted the Celtic knot on it, just as ancient as the snake symbol. Although the Celtic knot wasn't an unseelie symbol.

His eyes met hers. "Did you get these from the ruins?"

"Aye."

"If you have never been able to enter the unseelie plane before, I suspect one or both of the objects have brought us here. Take us back to our world, now."

"I tried. But when I thought of my castle, it brought us to this one."

He glanced around at the hall. "This is an unseelie great hall."

Footfalls sounded outside the great room. A number of footfalls. If he were to guess, Tiernan would think the number would amount to six men. Like those they had seen on the beach. Had they finally tracked the princess and him here?

A figure seemed to melt out of the walls through a secret passageway, he assumed. A woman about Ritasia's age, wearing a pale blue gossamer gown, her bright red hair loose about her shoulders, her green eyes wide, stared at them.

"You!" she shrieked, pointing to Ritasia in his lap.

He wondered how the unseelie seemed to know Ritasia. And it wasn't in a good way. Which also made him think of how she'd gotten herself incarcerated in the dragon fae dungeon. She was supposed to be the one keeping her brother and cousins out of trouble, but it seemed to him, she got herself into enough all on her own. And he was ready to take on the role of her protector, permanently, to see that she stayed *out* of trouble.

"Guards!" the wild-eyed unseelie screamed.

Tiernan quickly said, "Take us somewhere else, princess. Try the human plane."

The unseelie's eyes narrowed. "Princess? Guards!"

The footfalls encroaching on their claimed territory quickened into a run.

Ritasia hugged Tiernan tight as if she was afraid she would lose him in the transport, then closed her eyes. Mist again surrounded him in the black void of space as she clung to him, and he kept his hold on her just as tight. He felt the transport, the air around them shifting, changing, the warmth of her body heating his, but all he could think about was where they would land next.

When they settled in the new place, he glanced around, half expecting to be either on the unseelie beach again or in the castle somewhere else. But instead, he saw scant lights illuminating shops selling books and clothes and toys. They were in a human mall somewhere. The place was cast in shadows, closed for the night. He thought to find a hardware store and see if he could remove the iron band around his ankle, and then *he* would take them wherever they would be safe.

"All right, we are in the human plane," he said. "Remove the ring and medallion."

Her skin was too pale, and she looked unwell.

"Ritasia?" he asked, cradling her head in his hands.

"Fae travel," she managed to get out. "I'm so dizzy, I can barely see straight. Complicated, I'm sure, by whatever drug Duke Tully's healer gave me."

"All right. Let me remove them." He pulled the chain over her head, untangling it from her long silky hair and pocketed the medallion. But before he could remove the ring, they heard someone coming. Several people actually. If it had been a mall security guard, he imagined only one here on patrol at night.

Either the seelie fae were having sport in the mall tonight, or the unseelie fae had followed them here. With the way things were going, he suspected the latter.

He removed the ring from her finger and whispered, "Transport us now. To your castle."

She groaned and he had to hold her tight to keep her from collapsing. "Ritasia, just this one more time."

Suddenly, the footfalls were racing toward them, and he could see the guards that they had run across at the beach headed straight for them, their swords still out. They meant business.

"Now," he whispered.

And she transported them. One more time.

To a beach again. He groaned. But the sand looked whiter, not as course as it had been on the unseelie beach. Had they finally reached the seelie plane?

"Ritasia," he whispered, the soft, warm breeze whipping about them. "Take us to your home. To your castle. To the lion fae kingdom."

She opened her eyes, barely looked at him with sorrow

reflecting in them, glanced at the beach, grimaced, and then closed her eyes again. "South Padre Island," she whispered.

"Human world?" he asked. "Or your kingdom?" At least he hoped.

"Human."

His gut clenched with the notion that the unseelie would soon find them. "They'll follow us here. Take us to your home. To the seelie plane. Now, Ritasia."

He could see in the misty distance the shape of people taking form. "Now."

"I..."

"You *can* do it, my fairy princess." How he hated not being able to transport them himself. Fae travel never bothered him, thank the goddess. But he hated that she felt so bad and would have to do this again.

The next thing he knew, they were sitting in a cell of a dungeon. He would have laughed in frustration if their situation had not been so dire.

The door was most likely locked, and a sleepy prisoner stared at them through the bars of his own cell across the narrow passageway. Then grinned.

Tiernan frowned at the fae. But despite the dank, moldy smell of the place, he was relieved to sense only the scent of seelie fae. *Smelly* seelie fae. Unless somehow this was a dungeon where the unseelie kept those who managed to enter their world locked away.

Although since ancient times, he'd never heard of that happening. And he didn't smell any unseelie in the place.

"What is the princess doing with ye in a cell?" the fae suddenly asked, when he realized who was sitting on the king's lap while Tiernan sat on the only wooden platform used as a bed in the cell.

He knew her! The prisoner knew the princess! They had to be back at her castle.

She was again sleeping, and he sighed with relief. Hating to disturb her, he had to alert the queen her daughter was safely back at the castle of Denkar.

Tiernan shouted, "Guard! Guard!"

Ritasia stirred and frowned up at him, then closed her eyes and seemed to drift off again.

He would have the guard release them now and somehow, he had to destroy the ring and medallion. No one could know of their existence. It was too dangerous for anyone to have the ability to enter the unseelie plane and threaten the tentative peace that existed between them.

He frowned when he heard no guard approach.

The fae prisoner laughed. "The guard will not come down here in the dead of the night. But ye will remain here with me when he learns ye have taken the princess hostage in one of our cells."

So the man was of the lion fae himself.

Her people would know he had no thought to kidnap the princess when they saw Tiernan was wearing a fae iron manacle and couldn't transport anyone anywhere.

"What are you doing in here?" he asked the prisoner.

"Tried to steal a bauble from the dig site. Nothing the queen would have ever missed, but that would have given me a ton of gold when I pawned it off. Ye know how it is with these royals. They have everything and cannot give away a farthing to us poor folk."

"Have you ever tried working at an honest job?" the king asked, knowing the type in his own realm. Steal, murder, whatever they had to do before they would ever work at a real job.

The thief snorted. "Ye steal the princess, hoping for a ransom, eh? Only somehow yer fae abilities got clipped and here ye are, sitting pretty in a cell." He frowned at him. "Where did ye get those fancy clothes? Steal them, too?"

They were so dusty from the fine red clay in the dig site, Tiernan was surprised the man could tell they had been cut from the finest of cloth.

He supposed he wasn't getting out of here until the guard came to feed the prisoner in the morning. Only one narrow bed was available to sleep on, and he would have to share it with Ritasia. He wasn't sleeping on the filthy cold stone floor for anything. At least in the tunnels of the ancient fae castle, the rocky floor had only been dusty. He lay down on the hard plank and covered them with the sole moth-eaten, mildew-smelling blanket. "If you wake before the guard comes, please remove us from the cell and take us to a guest chamber," he whispered to her.

She nudged her head against his chest, her hair falling about him in a cascade of silk, as if she had agreed in her sleepy way.

A couple of hours later, a small slit of light shone through the slim arrow hole in the upper wall, and Tiernan knew the sun was coming up finally. With Ritasia nestled against his chest, sleeping soundly as he kept her wrapped in his arms, he'd managed to stay fairly warm and hoped he'd kept her so also in the drafty, dingy dungeon. The prisoner in the cell across from them had finally quit badgering him as to who he was and why he held the princess hostage, and why he was in the cell. He warned him it would not go well for Tiernan for having the princess in bed with him.

On the other hand, the prisoner looked like he wished their roles were reversed.

Then the prisoner, after a valiant effort of trying to watch them all night long, as if he would be the witness to tell all to the queen and maybe get a shortened sentence, finally fell asleep.

Blessedly.

The creaking of hinges sounded and Tiernan assumed the guard would be walking down the dark corridor before long. The guard would be startled to see a couple of new prisoners and try to figure that out, before he realized just who the one was. Tiernan was certain the man would be clueless as to who the king was. In any case, he assumed the guard would be irate to see him locked in an intimate embrace with the princess when he was not her husband.

But Tiernan wasn't waking her and setting her aside for propriety's sake. He had decided she would be his bride after all.

The hefty guard's bushy dark brown brows knit in a frown as he carried a torch in one hand, a bowl of slush in the other. He looked as though this job was just as disagreeable as the slop he would feed to the prisoner. The torchlight wavered as he approached the other man's cell, not even looking Tiernan and Ritasia's way. Then again, there really was no reason for the guard to do so. No one was supposed to be in the cell anyway.

He shoved the torch in an iron holder. Then tapped the bowl against the bars of the cell.

"Halaren, do you want to break yer fast or no', man?"

Tiernan suspected then that the prisoner must be an early riser usually, but with asking questions of Tiernan half the night, he'd worn himself out.

The man opened one bleary eye. Then both. His hair as crumpled as his brown clothes, he quickly sat up as if suddenly remembering his conversation with the king that night. Then his gaze shifted to Tiernan's as if he worried he might not be there, and he'd missed all the entertainment when the man and the princess had been discovered.

Tiernan gave him a smug smile.

The prisoner shouted, "Goddess save us! Did ye no' see the man with the princess? Holding her hostage all night, he was!"

The guard growled at the prisoner. "Ye no' be getting out of yer cell, feigning ye gone mad!"

"Nay. Over there." The prisoner motioned to Tiernan, offering a bigger smile now. "He has locked her into the cell with him."

The guard refused to look and passed the bowl of green slop through a slot in the iron door. "Eat or no'. Ain't my belly that'll go aching for it."

But despite acting as though he wouldn't look, the guard did as he turned around to amble off. "By the gods," the man growled, and came at the cell door, pulling out a dagger sheathed at his belt. "Unhand the princess, ye devil."

"You must address me as lord, my good man, as I am King Tiernan of the hawk fae kingdom. Princess Ritasia will be my wife. But for now...she sleeps."

The guard already had his keys out before the king finished speaking and stared slack-jawed at him through the bars of the cell.

"She has been missing. I heard tell ye had vanished as well."

"Aye, and we're back as you can see. Only Duke Tully clamped me in fae iron, and the princess was drugged and was only able to transport us here to this cell. I called out last night, but your friend there warned us that you wouldn't be visiting the dungeon in the middle of the night."

The guard quickly bowed and sheathed his weapon. "A thousand pardons, my lord. I'll get the shackle off ye, and I must tell the queen at once and..."

"If you just release us from the cell, that would be much appreciated."

"Aye, aye, of course, my lord."

But after the man unlocked the cell, he did remove the iron manacle from the king's ankle. "I'll let the queen know we have returned," Tiernan said.

"Aye, my lord." The guard stroked his scruffy dark chin whiskers and looked like he thought he was in dire trouble.

He would be, once the queen learned the king had hollered to be released and no one came to free him and her daughter. If a sick prisoner had called for help, he could have died before aid was given. And though the prisoner was a prisoner, he didn't look like he would be in here permanently. More as punishment for attempting to steal from the dig site and a warning to others to take heed.

King Tiernan had thought to walk up the stairs to the second floor of the keep where the great hall was, so that he would not startle too many of the dark fae, but it would take longer than he wished. He transported a sleeping Ritasia to the great hall and found it filled with courtiers breaking their fast that morning, hearing bits and pieces of conversation on how everyone wanted to put Duke Tully and his band in a deep grave and bury them forever, or drown him in the sea, or throw them in the dungeon and destroy the key.

But as soon as one pair of eyes saw him standing in the entryway carrying the princess, all eyes turned to see them, and conversation instantly ceased.

The queen rose shakily and shrieked, "How did you...what has happened? Ritasia!"

Tiernan strode toward the dais. "Duke Tully's maid gave her a healing and sleeping draught to help heal her broken arm. But I believe the number of times she transported us to the wrong locations because she was so disoriented had something to do with wearing her out. Unfortunately, I was wearing an iron manacle and could not use fae travel to bring us here."

"Take her to her chambers," the queen hastily commanded two of her knights.

When the one took her from Tiernan, he hated to give her up and gave the knight a look to take care with the lady. Two maids followed the men out of the hall.

She motioned to the physician to check the princess out also.

"Come, eat with us, my lord," the queen said, looking and sounding stricken still, her face pale, dark circles beneath her eyes. "And tell us everything. We knew Duke Tully had taken you both hostage, and I sent a messenger to the dragon fae king demanding your release, but—"

Tiernan wished to bathe first and change into fresh clothes, but the queen seemed so distraught, he had to speak with her about what had happened first.

But not about everything. Not how long they had been alone in the tunnels, nor of what they had discovered. He still had to destroy the medallion and ring.

When he sat beside the queen at the table, Prince Deveron was glowering at him. Probably because he knew he had been with his sister alone for hours.

"I'm ready to decide on a betrothal agreement," King Tiernan said, to put any gossip to rest. "I want Ritasia to be my wife."

8

The queen looked so surprised that King Tiernan would wish Ritasia as his bride, he wondered why. But then again, maybe it was because she didn't think he could see the princess as his queen, not after what had happened, both at the dinner the night before and the fiasco at the digs.

"We have to have Ritasia's agreement in this," Deveron said to his mother in a demanding tone. "You've always said she has the final say."

His mother waved her hand dismissively at the prince. "Because of the circumstances, which are beyond our control, the king has every right to ask for her hand, and I accept his offer wholeheartedly."

"But my lady mother...," Prince Deveron objected, still sounding fierce.

Tiernan liked Deveron. He was glad Ritasia had a brother who was so protective of her. He would welcome Deveron's visit to the hawk fae kingdom anytime.

"She won't object," Tiernan said, attempting to assure him that Ritasia would be willing to agree to the plan. At least he hoped she would be. He had every intention of making Ritasia his wife and ensuring she was happy. She *would* be his bride.

Mayhap he *was* a bit of a tyrant like his father after all.

"I must see Ritasia," Deveron said.

His mother opened her mouth to speak, and Tiernan thought she was going to object. He quickly said, "Please give Ritasia my best regards, Prince Deveron. And..." He paused, then pulled the princess's boots from where they were still tucked under his belt.

Deveron did not lessen his glower as he glanced at his sister's boots, yet when he met the king's gaze, a hint of dark admiration appeared in his eyes. And then Deveron took the boots, bowed to both his mother and the king, and vanished.

"Was it wise of you to permit my son to see her?" the queen asked wryly. "He might try to unduly influence her."

Tiernan cast her a knowing smile. "I wish to have the prince on my side. He would be a true friend and ally. He will see that I have caused no harm to come to the princess."

"And if she doesn't wish to wed you?"

Tiernan thought about that for a brief second. Then shook his head. "I believe her greatest fear will be to live so far away from her home. And she knows nothing of my people. With your permission, I will take her home with me and if she is agreeable to wed, we will send word."

Queen Irenis smiled. "'Tis a deal."

If only he could get Ritasia to go with him in the first place. Despite wanting Deveron's friendship as he could see how close brother and sister were, he didn't want Deveron's interference should he not like that Tiernan was taking her so far away.

At one of the lower tables, his advisor caught his eye and bowed his head to him in greeting, his expression one of concern. The rest of his men also bowed their heads to him, acknowledging his safe return. He was glad they appeared well and had not been thrown in the dungeon when he and Ritasia had disappeared. But he saw their worried expressions too. What would happen now if the princess did not agree to go with the tyrant king?

DEVERON PACED across Ritasia's bedchambers as the physician announced her arm nearly healed, and her maid stood nearly plastered against the wall too far away to be any good to anyone.

Ritasia looked so pale and innocent and young. Too young to marry a king and move so far away. "Aye, but she is not awake. Wake her."

"My lord?"

"Do it. Now. Her fate is at stake."

The physician stroked his gray beard, shifting his worried gaze from Ritasia to Deveron. "But, Prince Deveron, I do not know what drug they gave the princess. If I give her something else, it must be something to counteract it. But I do not know what would. Anything I might give her could worsen the effect."

"All right," Deveron conceded, hating to. "What about the rest of her?"

"The rest of her, my lord?"

"She is still…" Deveron frowned. "Forget it. I will ask my sister when she wakes. If she ever wakes. Are you sure it's not something like when the winged fae, Princess Serena, drugged my cousin, Niall?"

"I would not know for certain. And if it was, then Duke Tully's healer would have to give Princess Ritasia the antidote."

"All right. You may go."

"Yes, my lord." The physician looked enormously relieved and hurried out of the bedchambers.

Two knights guarded the door as if they were needed *now*, and Ritasia's maid, Melissina, stood quietly, holding up the wall with her back, wringing her hands.

"What is the matter with you?" Deveron snapped. He still couldn't believe the hawk king had led his sister astray, they had been lost in the ancient tunnels, and then he allowed them both to be captured by Duke Tully's men. If the hawk king wished his sister as his wife, he would have to take better care of her! "The princess is here, safe and sound, and—"

"She was having a nightmare about the unseelie. They tried to come for her and the king."

Deveron stared at the blue-eyed, middle-aged blonde, not believing she was usually given to flights of hysteria over another's dreams, then he dismissed her concern. "It was just the effect of the drug. Leave us."

"But the queen said I was not to leave the princess's side."

"I'm seeing my sister and she needs no chaperone. Unlike last night," he growled, despite knowing that it wasn't Melissina's fault as the queen herself had ordered that she not accompany the princess in the gardens while she walked with the king.

Which his sister did not do! She should have had three maids with her at all times. And a guard or two!

"Aye, my lord. I'm sorry, my lord."

Melissina quickly curtsied, but before she could flee the room, Deveron said, "Better prepare yourself for a trip."

Her eyes widened. Before she got the wrong impression and thought she was being dismissed from court, he quickly added, "It seems Ritasia will be seeing the hawk fae kingdom. And you will accompany her at all times while she is there."

Melissina fainted dead away.

RITASIA WOKE to the sound of birds chirping outside her chamber and the fragrance of fresh roses from the royal greenhouse scenting the air next to her bed, momentarily disoriented. The last place she vaguely remembered being was the dungeon with Tiernan, her sleep disturbed by the fae who had tried to steal the queen's comb from the digs.

She glanced at the flowers and saw Deveron sitting in a chair nearby, studying her, his brows knit tightly in a worry frown. As soon as he caught her eye, he rose from the chair and moved to the bed. "Are you all right?" he asked in a rush.

She loved her brother and was glad to see him worrying over her, but she wanted to see the king. Was *he* all right?

"Oh, aye." She sat up in bed and Deveron hurried to move pillows behind her back as if he was a well-trained lady's maid, something she'd never seen him do. "Thank you." She frowned. "Where is King Tiernan?"

"Breaking his fast and making marriage arrangements with Mother for your hand in marriage." He sounded annoyed but observed her to see her reaction as if wanting to know which way he should view this—as good news or bad.

Ritasia's mouth gaped wide, then she clamped her lips shut. So he wanted her, did he? Without asking her? Or at least mentioning it to her first?

She touched her injured arm, but it appeared to be properly healed, and she felt no more pain.

"What happened last night? The whole story," Deveron insisted.

She explained everything, except about the medallion and ring. She vaguely remembered being so drugged she barely could recall seeing the unseelie fae or the feeling of terror she had experienced when she couldn't quickly move Tiernan and her somewhere safe. And then he'd removed the medallion and ring from her person and...they had to be destroyed!

What had he done with them? Where was he now?

"Ritasia, what are you not telling me?" her brother asked, his dark brows still furrowed.

She shook her head. Had her mother known of the artifacts and wanted them so she could enter the unseelie world?

"Was he a gentleman?" Deveron persisted.

Then, she saw how he was ready to take up the sword against Tiernan. She quickly said, "Aye, always. He only had my safety and comfort in mind, at all times."

Deveron studied her for a moment, then nodded as if he believed her. "Why does he want to marry you then?"

Ritasia scowled at her brother. "Probably because he finds me witty and charming and irresistible."

Deveron snorted.

"Well, *you* don't have to marry me. Thank the goddess."

"Do you wish to go?"

She didn't say anything for a long time. She'd always been close to her brother. At times inseparable. But they'd changed. He wanted to be with Alicia now. She needed someone to love of her own.

Yes, she wanted to go and see for herself all there was to see of the hawk fae kingdom. She wanted to see how his people would treat her and how he treated them. If he truly was a tyrant, she wouldn't marry him. But she really would miss her mother, Deveron, his betrothed, Alicia, and her cousins if she chose to marry Tiernan.

"Ritasia?"

"Aye, I do. But it does not mean I will marry him for sure."

Deveron took a deep, settling breath.

She smiled.

"Do you truly care for him?"

"Aye." She didn't hesitate to answer her brother then. With her, Tiernan was protective and gentle, demanding, but only in as much as he wanted to keep her safe. And they had an unspoken secret between them that they needed to resolve right away.

"Just as you care for Alicia, I care for Tiernan."

Deveron didn't say anything, but he looked as though he was coming to terms with this. "Will you join us for the rest of the meal, then?"

She shook her head. "I want a bath first. If you could have something brought up for me to eat, I will be forever grateful."

"Aye, so be it." Looking much less pensive then when she had first seen him, Deveron kissed her cheek, then left her alone.

After bathing in soothing lavender-scented water, she barely had time to dress in a burgundy gown, wanting to show Tiernan she could look like a lady when she was of a mind to do so, when her mother stalked into her bedchamber. She knew she would get a scolding.

Her mother's eyes were narrowed, but dark circles shadowed them and so Ritasia imagined her mother had been more than worried about her last night. Ritasia opened her mouth to offer an apology as she had not had any intention of scaring her mother like that.

"I meant for you to see the king at various social activities where you could get to know each other in a courtly and honorable way. I did not expect this of you, young lady."

"This" meaning going to the digs at night unchaperoned with the king.

Ritasia wanted to say that anyone could go to the gardens on a date but going to the digs showed just how... noble the king could be to allow her to do as she pleased when she was certain he didn't wholly like the idea.

"Aye, my lady mother," she said instead.

"Your brother told me that you are agreeable to accompanying the king to his kingdom, which is good because after what you pulled, you would be going no matter what."

Ritasia didn't believe her mother would really send her if she cried and fussed and begged her not to.

When Ritasia didn't respond quickly enough, her mother said, "You are agreeable, are you not?"

Glad to know her mother still had Ritasia's best interests at heart, Ritasia smiled. "Of course, my lady mother. I'm curious about his kingdom."

The queen sighed.

"But if he treats his people cruelly or me, even, I will say no to the marriage arrangement."

Her mother nodded. "As you wish, daughter. Is your arm really all right?"

"Healed."

Her mother sat down on the chair next to the bed, her eyes narrowed again. "He wants to take you home right away. This afternoon even."

"This afternoon?" Ritasia squeaked.

"Aye. He didn't want to leave his kingdom without his rule for too long and it has been nearly two weeks."

"Oh." She hadn't expected that. Maybe that he would want to enjoy her company for a few days here first, like her mother had initially planned. But to leave so all of a sudden like that? "Nothing untoward happened between us," Ritasia hastened to say.

Her mother smiled then, her concerned expression melting away. "I did not think so, Ritasia, or you would have told your brother right away. And he would have informed me." Then she sobered again. "Deveron will wed Alicia, if they can ever quit having these bouts of...well, I don't know what is causing dissention between them." She paused, looking to Ritasia to fill her in.

But Ritasia wouldn't tell her Micala was causing all the difficulty by seeing the human girl. When Ritasia wouldn't enlighten her, her mother nodded. "But he will wed, and you will be alone."

So that's why her mother had been foisting all these suitors on her. She had been afraid Ritasia would be distraught or too lonely when Deveron was gone, not that her mother was tired of her or wanted someone else to be responsible for her.

"I'm glad you feel some fondness for the king. That's how your father and I began our relationship, you know."

Ritasia snorted. "I doubt you and he were lost in ancient fae tunnels and taken prisoner by dragon fae on your first date."

At her comment, her mother smiled broadly, making her look ten years younger, although she always looked young. "You would be surprised."

Ritasia waited to hear what had happened to her mother and father on their first date. Neither had ever discussed such a thing with her. Had they told Deveron? She doubted it.

"Well?" Ritasia said, when her mother looked as though she was lost in the memories of her youth.

Again, her mother smiled. "I was nearly as willful as you."

Ritasia raised her brows.

"Well, as willful. Which is why I cannot fault you too much for your wayward ways. I was angry with my mother because she wanted me to wed a lord I wasn't interested in. But he had wealth and power and connections and would be a king of the sphinx fae in his own right. He was a bore. So I slipped onto a boat heading for one of the islands, and we encountered a terrible storm. I refused to fae travel back home, knowing my mother might marry me off to the future king without hesitation for disobeying her."

"She would have been so grateful you were home, do you not think?"

Queen Irenis scoffed under her breath. "She would have married me off to prove she was right. The lord I was to marry would have been furious with me and well, I decided to take my chances with the ship and the storm. Not a good choice. At the time, at least. The ship broke up on the rocks, taking on water so quickly, that it was beneath the sea minutes later, and I found myself clinging to a piece of driftwood, bruised, battered, and bloodied."

"What happened to the others? The crew?"

"I'm sure they fae traveled out of there."

"Why didn't you fae travel back home?"

"I hadn't been gone long enough for my mother to even have noticed. If I returned then, she would have dismissed my concerns and married me off anyway. She wasn't about to give me a choice."

"But...how is this the same as my being with King Tiernan?"

"It wasn't quite the same, but our first date was similar, in some respects. A larger ship than ours had noted our sinking and had come to see if anything of value was drifting about in the storm-roughened seas. They didn't expect to find a half-drowned dark fae clinging to a remnant of the ship."

"So Father was on the ship?"

"He was the captain." Something akin to a wicked gleam lighted her mother's eyes.

"He was not a king," Ritasia guessed.

"Nay. He was a pirate captain. Privateer, he informed me. He rescued me, which I thought so romantic, only he wished to ransom me to my mother. And I told him to go right ahead, that a future king wanted me for a wife, and he could ask him for money too. He threatened for weeks to ransom me, and for weeks I told him to do so. But in the end, he decided he couldn't live without me, offered for my hand in marriage, and when I finally became queen, he was my king."

"He had no royal blood?"

"Oh, aye. He was a duke but was being paid handsomely by one kingdom or another to strip the wealth from ships that belonged to their enemies. He gave up his pirating ways to be with me though. I believe only because our kingdom was so near the sea."

"Nothing to do with you, though," Ritasia said, smiling, loving her father all the more. She'd wished she'd known this about him and would have asked him for days on end about his pirating adventures before he had died. He had seemed so staid. She couldn't imagine him commanding a ship and stealing goods from other fae kingdoms. Or rescuing her mother and keeping her and threatening to ransom her.

"Oh, aye, he loved me all right, from the moment he saw me floating in the sea. He said he thought I was a mermaid as no fae in their right mind would have remained where I was and not fae transported home. In truth, I think he didn't want to send me home to face a marriage I didn't want. And we grew on each other with each passing day." Her mother took a deep breath. "I would never force you into a marriage you didn't want, you know."

"Thank you, my lady mother." She wrapped her arms around her mother and gave her a sincere hug.

Her mother returned the embrace, then pulled away and looked very serious now. "You will need to have your servants pack your things. You will fly out of Dallas since fae travel would take too long and you couldn't handle it, I'm afraid, from what the king said."

This afternoon. She wouldn't even have time to say goodbye to Deveron's betrothed.

"You'll take Melissina with you and two of my knights will go along to watch over you." The queen didn't say anything more as she walked over to the window and looked out. Then she turned and said, "Melissina told me that you spoke of seeing unseelie."

Ritasia was so startled by the statement, she hesitated as she tried to come up with a plausible explanation. "In a dream. I was dreaming."

"We see them in the human world from time to time, though we avoid each other."

"Aye. I'm sure I was thinking of a time when I had seen some and the experience had manifested itself in a dream."

"What about the one you were nearly having words with at South Padre Island?"

"That might have triggered the dream," Ritasia said quickly.

"You found nothing in the castle when you left the king in the wine cellar and before the floor collapsed?" Her mother was giving her one of her discerning looks, waiting for a reaction. Any reaction that would clue her in as to the truth. Did she know about the ring? The medallion? Had the king told her about them?

"Many things," Ritasia said vaguely, not lying. "They wanted to be left where they were. The queen's personal memories belonged with her burial chamber."

Because that's what it was like, except the queen was not there. Although she deliberately had left out the part about the items that did *not* remain behind.

Still studying her, Queen Irenis said, "In our archives, scholars have found papers that state that Queen Minova and over a hundred of her people were taken prisoner in the unseelie kingdom of Na."

Ritasia stared at her mother in disbelief. "Taken prisoner." She barely breathed. "Would they still be alive?"

"Oh, aye. We live very long lives. If they allowed them to live, that is."

Ritasia felt sick to her stomach. The queen's bed had been turned down for her, but she'd never returned to the castle, never again slept in her bed.

"Purportedly, the queen had discovered an artifact that allowed her to break through the fabric separating the seelie and unseelie planes."

"Break through?" Again, a feeling of uneasiness swamped Ritasia.

"More than that, with her power, it was conjectured that she had actually created the object."

How could the queen have done such a thing?

"But why? We've always been taught that we shouldn't ever acknowledge the unseelie when we see them, and they ignore us."

"Aye. We believe that the unseelie had magic she wished to learn from. To ever break into the unseelie world was forbidden. Not after the fighting between them over nine centuries ago. It was thought neither side could ever win, and if they weren't careful, each side would wipe out the other's existence forever and the fae worlds would no longer exist."

"But she went into their realm anyway?"

"And stole one of their medallions. Several times, she slipped in, stole some aspect of their magic, and returned to her own kingdom. But one of the unseelie saw her. For years, they watched for her, waiting for when she might show up in the human plane or waiting for her to return to the unseelie lands, the only way they could meet up with her. When she returned to the human world, she had left the artifacts at her own castle, and they had no way of going to the seelie court. So they took her hostage. Every fae who went in search of her, met her same fate until those who were left behind moved on. But one wrote about what had happened and our scholars finally deciphered it."

"She was evil then?" Ritasia asked.

"Mayhap. Mayhap not. She might have just been terribly curious, insatiable, bored. Too much so for her own good."

She thought the look her mother gave her said she was just like the queen. "Could anyone rescue her? If anyone had the means, should they?"

Her mother's eyes narrowed. "Nay. Her kingdom is gone. She has lived for too many years among the unseelie. Or she may be dead."

"Is that what you were looking for?" Ritasia asked.

"The artifact must be destroyed. If it falls into the wrong hands, our worlds could very well be at war again. Do you understand the seriousness of this, Ritasia?" her mother asked, ignoring her question.

"Aye."

"Good. Then pack for your trip, daughter, and may your journey be safe."

Her mother normally would have told her to have a *pleasant* journey, so telling her to be safe gave Ritasia a chill.

Her mother gave her another hug and a kiss, then left the room. That's when Ritasia noticed her dusty clothes that she'd worn to the dig were gone. To be washed. But also to be searched? She would find the queen's comb that Ritasia should have left in her mother's treasure vault.

An hour later, packed and ready to go to a new world, Ritasia joined Tiernan and the rest of her people in the great hall to say farewell. She tried not to be anxious and noted the concern in Tiernan's expression as they readied to leave her mother and brother and cousins at the Denkar castle where they would transport to the airport with a small group who would travel with them.

Queen Irenis said, "Keep her safe, King Tiernan. If...," she hesitated, then continued, "the unseelie can find you whenever you're in the human world. Watch your backs."

Deveron frowned at his mother, and Ritasia knew her brother must not know what secret wisdom her mother was trying to impart to them. But Tiernan knew. He squeezed Ritasia's hand to reassure her, then said, "I will keep her safe."

She noted he was wearing his sword and his dirk also. She had her own dagger too.

And she wondered then if this was the reason he and her mother wished to remove her from the kingdom of the Denkar and send her halfway around the world.

Where she might be safer.

But when they arrived at the airport in Dallas, she noted thirty or so armed knights also escorted Tiernan, his men, Melissina, and her. Ritasia didn't believe it was a welcome send off from her kingdom to honor the hawk fae king. Rather that her mother believed they would have trouble from the unseelie who happened to be at the airport today.

All of the fae were invisible, though Tiernan had explained how he had wanted to obtain a seat for her in first class so that she didn't have to deal with humans who might sit in the fae-chosen seats. But he didn't say why they had to remain invisible, and she didn't ask. She was afraid it had all to do with the unseelie should they join them on their flight today.

But it wouldn't be easy for the unseelie to be able to spread out so thin, to watch anywhere that Ritasia and the king might travel, though she suspected they would be watching South Padre Island, so far south in Texas that it wouldn't have any consequences for her here in Dallas. But she'd been in South Padre Island when they'd seen her there, and the witch of a redheaded unseelie had had words with her, so she figured they would be watching that area in particular. Maybe the mall the king had told her she'd taken them to. That had been in San Antonio, so again, too far from Dallas to cause concern.

Relieved, she saw no unseelie in the terminal area and she and the king, her maid, Melissina, and the king's men boarded the airplane. But what she couldn't believe was that her mother's guard entered it also. And took seats throughout the plane.

"My mother said nothing about sending guards with us," she whispered to the king as he ushered her into one of the first-class seats. She was afraid Tiernan would be offended, believing that her mother did not trust him or his people with Ritasia's safety once she was at the hawk fae kingdom.

"For your safety, princess," Tiernan said, quite congenially, sitting next to her. "They will return home to your people after we arrive at my castle."

"Do you still have the ring and medallion?" she asked.

"Aye. At least one of them is a magical artifact that can transport the wearer through the fabric that separates the two courts. Mayhap both are magical. They need to be destroyed."

He watched her reaction closely as if trying to see if she believed as he did, or if she wanted to keep them for herself. Or even give them to her mother.

"How will we successfully destroy them?" She wanted to assure him that she only wished to get rid of the objects permanently.

"Two of my people have the ability to destroy the magic without demolishing the object carrying the magical properties. But Sophia can make it appear as though the magic is still captured within."

"Why would that be important?"

"The unseelie will come for these, princess. If they know the magic has been destroyed, they might fight us. Or not. If they believe they are still magical, they may return with them to their own court and try to discover why the objects no longer work."

"What if Queen Minova is trapped in the unseelie world? Imprisoned as long as she lives?" Ritasia still had it in mind that she would like to free the queen and her people.

Tiernan let out his breath in a weary sigh. "She is trapped. We cannot risk going there to free her and cause a rift between the worlds. It is very much like playing with fire. Get too close and you risk all. She made her choice."

"And her people?"

"Unfortunately, they did too." He looked thoughtfully at her, then took her hand in his and gently said, "How did you end up in the dragon fae's dungeon?"

She raised her brows. She hadn't expected him to bring that up again. "I was trying to save my cousin Niall. He had fallen head over heels for a winged fae, and she was seeing some knight of the dragon fae at the Renaissance fair in Waxahachie. I had to learn what I could to try and stop him from getting his heart broken."

At that, Tiernan smiled and shook his head. "I doubt you could have stopped that."

"You're right, of course. It was already too late for him. Then the dragon fae knight ordered me sent off to the dungeon at once. But all ended well."

Tiernan grunted at that and squeezed her hand as if he'd wished he'd been there to protect her and she would never have ended up in any dungeon, dragon or otherwise. Well, except for her own dungeon. She'd heard the guard who had not come when Tiernan called for their release had been fired and banished from the kingdom. Her mother would not tolerate the mistreatment of prisoners, unless to get a confession. But once they were serving their time, she expected them to be cared for, if they needed it.

"And the unseelie fae who recognized you at the great hall in the unseelie world?" he asked.

Despite how out of it she had been when she was sitting on Tiernan's lap in the great hall of the unseelie fae, she should have known he would ask why the unseelie knew her and was so hostile. She had really wanted to say something in retort to the haughty woman, but as muddled as her head had been, all she could concentrate on was Tiernan's urgent coaxing to get them out of there. And hoping she would do it right.

She tried not to squirm under the king's scrutiny, felt her face warm considerably, and knew he noticed it also. She didn't think he would appreciate it if she told him she was going to look for a male human's companionship for the afternoon, found one, in fact, and was about to come to daggers with the unseelie fae who targeted him too. But how could she explain why the unseelie hated her so much, otherwise?

"I was there, seeking to help my cousin Micala, who, I'm afraid, has lost his heart to a human girl. Deveron ordered him not to see her. I like Cassie, and I planned to meet her in South Padre Island instead of my cousin, and well, let her down gently, that Micala wasn't coming to see her. Ever."

At least that sounded...noble.

Tiernan caressed her hand with his thumb, nodding. "You do indeed seek to save your cousins from their own folly." Then he took a deep breath and added, "But it doesn't explain what occurred between the unseelie and you."

She wanted to clear her throat, give her a moment more to think of her answer, then she figured what the goddess? She was a fae and fae were known to play with the humans. If he didn't like it, so be it.

"I saw a human that I fancied could buy me an ice cream sundae."

Tiernan's mouth curved up ever so slightly.

She quickly continued. "I had to see Cassie in the ice cream parlor. So I figured it would be nice to have someone buy me a hot fudge sundae."

"A human male."

She shrugged, couldn't help smiling, somewhat brought on by his amused expression. He glanced down at the gown she wore and looked back up at her face. She wasn't sure what she saw there, admiration, jealousy maybe, that some human male might have taken an interest in her. He hadn't said one thing about how she looked while wearing one of her prettiest fae gowns, her hair coiled in curls on her head, emerald encrusted combs keeping the curls in place. She wondered if he preferred her dressed in a man's tunic and beeches, for all the compliments she'd gotten from him.

"And the unseelie?"

"After I saw him, she came back to target him. She nearly ran into me when I first arrived, seeing me before I saw her. She had it out for me from the beginning."

"Fae spite."

"Certainly. What had I ever done to her?"

"Targeted the same human male on the beach." He again looked at her gown, then said, "I would hate to know what you were wearing for the human to see."

She cleared her throat at that. "Deveron came and forced me to leave. I didn't even get to say anything to Cassie."

"Or spend the afternoon with the human male." He studied her for a moment more, and she knew the way his gaze focused on hers he wished to ask another question and so she waited. "What were you wearing?" he finally asked.

This time she couldn't contain her smile, although she truly didn't want to say. But she thought he might be a bit jealous. "A bathing suit."

"A bikini?"

"Not as skimpy as the one the unseelie was wearing," she said.

Tiernan's hand brushed her arm with a gentle caress. "When it warms up, you will wear this bikini for me."

"What if I didn't bring it with me?"

Tiernan's eyes sparkled with intrigue. "I'll buy you another, my choice."

She could imagine him getting her one as skimpy as the bikini the unseelie had worn. But she wasn't going for it.

"So Deveron forced you to go home and...?"

"I learned I was to be at the dig site, and I was forbidden to go to South Padre Island for a month."

"Longer than that," Tiernan promised.

She ignored what he was hinting at—a marriage and she would not be able to visit the island at whim any longer. Although she could see where that might be prudent, given who was probably waiting there for her. Probably any of the dark fae visiting the area would have to have an armed escort now.

Ritasia leaned back against the plane seat, didn't remark about his comment, but dove back into a more immediate problem. "We have to make it right by eliminating the power within the ring and medallion, although I suspect the medallion has no power. Just the ring." She gave a bitter laugh. "I thought that nothing of value would ever be found in the castle ruins. I never expected to find a device that could create a war between the unseelie and seelie courts."

He slipped his hand around hers and gave a squeeze of reassurance.

And here she'd wondered what to do with herself that could be adventurous and dangerous, thinking that she couldn't get herself into too much trouble unless she was trying to get her brother or cousins out of their own difficulties.

None of them had ever gotten into a mess of this magnitude... ever!

9

Ritasia was tired by the time she arrived at the court of the hawk fae after the long human flight that went through the night. Earlier that morning, everyone came out to see her in their finery, although she had wanted to sleep as she couldn't on the plane. Though she'd worn a lovely gown that fluttered as a warm breeze floated through the windows of the great hall, the rich fabric was a little wrinkled so at the very least, she'd wanted to change. But she knew she could not do just as she wished, not in Tiernan's court, and truly she wanted to please him. He didn't seem to want to let her out of his sight at the moment while he showed her off to those who appeared high in the royal chain and those of the lowliest servants.

He seemed so proud of her as he presented her to his people that she was truly surprised. She hadn't expected all the fanfare, not when she wasn't married to him.

And though she knew he wanted her to be his wife, she hadn't expected him to be so...enamored with her. Surely after the fiasco she'd caused, he was sure to believe, before long, she would be in another mess. Then again, maybe he thought he would be able to ensure she didn't get herself into trouble like that again. Well, for a while she probably wouldn't. Not until she learned all she could about the place. There would be time enough for adventures galore.

He leaned down and whispered in her ear, which sent a tingle of heat cascading through her blood, "Your room is being prepared as we speak, no time to get word to the staff before we arrived."

So that was the reason she couldn't have freshened up a bit right away.

Melissina stood nearby, looking as though she could fall asleep on her feet.

"What about the ring and medallion?" she whispered back, and the crowd watching them smiled or murmured comments, probably believing she and the king were whispering sweet sentiments to each other.

"Later," he whispered back, then smiled at his people.

Her skin heated at the notion that everyone watched them as much as in her own court. Only in her own court, she at least knew her people and they knew her.

Several women approached her in a timid way and curtseyed and wished her and the king well, their eyes on her, not on the king. Were they afraid of him?

She greeted them as if they would all be her best friends, yet she saw the aloofness that persisted.

Were they afraid of her?

He motioned for a lad of about fourteen to come to her. She recognized he was human at once as he had no fae aura, no gold circles around his eyes, no scent of the fae, and her hackles rose. Her own people hadn't taken humans into service for centuries, though many of the fae kingdoms thought nothing of it.

But she'd never considered the hawk fae kingdom would have human servants. To the king's credit, the young man was the only one she had seen among the fae here so far.

"This is Romero. He will be your page and will carry your

messages to me whenever we are separated, and you need to speak with me."

The boy was fitted in the finest forest green tunic and breeches, his long dark hair curling about his shoulders, his blue eyes bright with intrigue. "My lady," the boy said, bowing low.

She belatedly curtseyed once she realized she had not done so. She couldn't help it. She was still so startled to see him here. "Is he mine to do with as I see fit?" she asked Tiernan.

He looked a little taken aback by the question. "What exactly had you in mind, my lady?"

"We do not keep humans in my kingdom. I want him returned to the human world."

Tiernan's expression darkened a bit. She realized, too late as usual, that she should have waited for a better time to voice her displeasure. His people lived differently than hers, and she would have to get used to it, or choose not to stay here at all.

"We will discuss this later. *Privately.*" He seemed highly annoyed, curbing his temper just for his people as he took her arm and moved her toward the dais where the royals would sit at the high table.

She took a deep breath. She wanted the boy returned to the human world. But for now, she would pretend to be the princess guest who was happy to be here and took the seat where Tiernan directed her. She figured she could manage to get through one meal without causing a scene between them.

Once everyone had a glass of red wine, he proposed a toast. "To the woman who shall be my wife. *Soon.*"

Oh, no he couldn't have said that. Before this, when he'd announced who she was, he'd called her their honored guest from the lion fae kingdom. He had made no mention she would be his wife, which was the way she wished it. For now, she had to learn all there was to observe about his kingdom. The good and the bad. She would see just how things worked out before she made up her mind whether she was staying here or not. But the fae in his court seemed thrilled their king had finally found his betrothed.

When he sat next to her, she noted her guards were seated with Melissina at one of the lower tables. The human boy was gone. He was probably sitting with the lowest servants in the kitchen or elsewhere.

Maybe Tiernan didn't want her to see Romero and insist on speaking about him further. But she had no intention of doing so. Not at the meal. She would not make another scene.

Instead, she said to Tiernan, "I do not recall meeting Sophia, your mage. Is she here? I was hoping we could have her dispel the magic on the jewelry however she does such a thing and then—"

"You have no need to worry about that. I will take care of it," Tiernan said shortly, and she thought he was still annoyed with her over her comments concerning Romero.

Fine. He could be irritated with her all he wanted. But the ring and the snake medallion were hers from her mother's dig site, and they didn't belong to the hawk fae king, nor his people.

The first portion of the meal had been served, although she wasn't hungry. She poked at the soup with her spoon but didn't take a bite.

He watched her for a few minutes, then finally said, "Do you always play with your food?"

She turned to scowl at him. "Do you always dictate everything? Even how someone eats or doesn't eat at a meal?" She hadn't meant for the ring around her eyes to glow gold, but she saw them reflected in his eyes.

He finally took a deep breath, still looking angered and said, "Eat or do not eat. It is up to you."

"Where is the boy?"

"Romero may look like a young man, but he is a couple centuries old, my lady."

She stared at him blankly.

"He cannot return to his home, to the people he knew. This is his home and has been forever. He was so young when the fae brought him here, he doesn't even know the human world."

She'd never considered such a thing. She gathered her wits and asked, "Why does he not eat with us?"

"I believe he feels you do not wish him to serve you."

"Me? Are you saying you did not have him sent away? Where does he usually eat? Somewhere hidden from the rest of your court? And now it is my fault?"

"He normally sits where your maid is seated," Tiernan said darkly.

Ritasia felt very small then and wanted to rectify the situation with the "boy." She took a deep breath and said, "Where is Romero? I'll go and speak with him."

"Nay, you will not," Tiernan said, with a hint of humorless laughter in his response. "You will be my queen and you will remain seated, eating or not eating as you so choose, until I say so. After that, we will take a courtly walk in the gardens and by then, your guest chambers will be ready for you to retire to at your leisure."

She considered rising from her seat and stalking out of the hall to show Tiernan just what she thought of his ruling her. She was his guest! Nothing more. And if he thought to treat her this way when she was his queen, forget that.

But she had to speak with Romero, and she had to find the ring and medallion. They were her responsibility, not Tiernan's.

She was pretty certain Tiernan would stop her if she tried to walk out on the meal on him without his permission, so she did what any good fae princess who was pissed off would do. She fae transported right out of the great hall, wishing to be in the gardens, and hoped she would end up on a path and not on the...top of a hedge maze. One that's shrubs were so stiff and compact, she sat right on top of them, way up high. Which was just the problem with wishing to transport somewhere that a fae hadn't visited before. She could have ended up in a pond in the gardens, or somewhere else even more disagreeable. The maze must have towered fifteen feet, and she wondered just what they fed their plants here.

She supposed her knights and Melissina would be frantic to see she had vanished from the great hall, which would have revealed she was perturbed with the king and would not abide his company a moment longer. His own people would either be silent in horror, or speaking in such a torrent, wondering what had happened to their illustrious guest.

The king? He was probably ready to kill her. He probably wasn't ready to send her home yet though.

Well, most likely not, and still save face.

She meant to transport to the golden brick path, but when she tried, she didn't move. Not an inch. What was wrong with her?

She tried again. But again, she had no luck. She stared at the ground. She couldn't get down from here without breaking her neck. She had never heard of anyone being able to cast a manacle spell on anyone without them being within sight.

No one was out here but the birds, bees, and a multitude of butterflies. And one dark fae princess stuck on top of a hedge maze.

TIERNAN REALLY DIDN'T WANT his bride-to-be to see how angry he was that she had left him alone at the beginning of the meal in front of all his courtiers. He would not make excuses to his people for her behavior. He wanted to go after her, shake her, and make her understand she could not behave in this way. Not if she was going to be his queen.

And yet, her flagrant disregard for his rules was what made him love her even more. He had to understand how different her people lived, how free-spirited she was, and he had to make allowances.

He was not a tyrant king, although right now he was feeling like locking her in a fae collar and making her stay by his side when he desired it of her.

The next best thing was calling Sophia forth and giving her a whispered command, "Stop all fae travel within the castle and extending out for one hundred miles beyond."

She was extremely capable of the task, and she curtseyed, then he knew she did her duty.

For the princess's safety and his peace of mind, he would not allow Ritasia to fae transport anywhere. When she came to her senses, after trying to walk all over this huge kingdom in search of Romero, she would finally return to the hall. Or seek out Tiernan wherever he might go, following the meal. For he was certain as determined and stubborn as she was, she would not return soon.

Everyone in the hall waited for his word. He thanked Sophia, and she went back to her seat. With a dark scowl on his face, one of Ritasia's knights finally rose, then walked over to the head table. "We are to watch the princess at all times, King Tiernan."

"She is safe, Sir Conklin. She can only walk wherever she wishes to go, so she will not go far."

"But—"

"Enjoy your meal. You may search for her afterward. She wishes to speak with her page. That is all. She will return before long."

The knight did not look like he believed it. But he didn't have a lot of choice and returned to his seat where he explained what the king had said to him to the other dark fae knight and her maid. They all looked at the king with a mixture of disbelief and irritation. Their conversation began again in earnest, and Tiernan believed as soon as he ended the meal, the three of them would be off, searching for the princess. But they would have to do so on foot.

The conversation had died down to a mere lull, like it had at Ritasia's court. He was beginning to think that wherever the princess took her meal, the people would be more fascinated with her, than with their own dinner companions and conversation. They probably also didn't wish to miss anything that occurred at the head table if anything more newsworthy were to occur.

Tiernan sliced up a piece of partridge, though he was no longer hungry, and though his advisor tried to speak to him about the wedding date and such, Tiernan only half listened to him. He couldn't help but watch the entryway to the great hall and hoped Ritasia would come to her senses. Or that she would speak with Romero, realize the human was happy where he was, and she would come back to sit beside Tiernan for the rest of the meal. Maybe even eat a bite or two. And look as though she was happy to be his bride-to-be.

When the next course arrived, he said to Lord Srenton, who had lapsed into silence, "Where would Romero be if he does not take his meal with us?"

"The kitchen, mayhap, my lord. Beyond that, I wouldn't know. His chamber below stairs, mayhap."

"Have them searched."

"And if the princess is in either location?"

King Tiernan raised his brows. "If she is in the kitchen with him, I wish to know this. If she is in his *chamber*..."

His advisor waited.

Tiernan frowned. "Send her to her chambers and have a guard posted, then let me know."

"Aye, my lord."

When Lord Srenton rose from the table, Tiernan stared up at him. "I did not mean for you to have the task."

"I would wish it to be me who finds the lady, and not some servant who would gossip to the rest of the court, my king."

"So be it."

Of course, everyone watched his advisor leave the great hall, and everyone had to know he was searching for the princess. Tiernan was certain his people could not wait for him to end the meal so *they* could look for the princess. But Tiernan had no intention of ending the meal early while his advisor searched and hopefully located the princess himself first and gave him the news.

RITASIA CONTEMPLATED CLIMBING down the shrub she was sitting upon as she'd been here forever, no matter how many times she'd tried to transport herself down and couldn't. She didn't want to wait until the meal ended and have any of the king's people find her up here. Her own, wouldn't be so bad. They knew her well enough. But his people...

She took another annoyed breath. She thought to call out, but she figured everyone was at the meal or someone would be passing through the gardens at some point. Or at least some would congregate somewhere out of doors, and she would hear them.

Which was when she heard running footfalls and a child's laughter. And then another.

She hadn't seen any children in the great hall, and she assumed the king didn't allow them to eat with the adults. But now, here a couple of them were, racing through the gardens.

She didn't want to alarm them, or really call attention to herself way high up above, but she didn't have much of a choice if she wanted to get down from here sooner than later. She could only see down one maze lane or crawling gingerly across the top, then looking over to the other side, that maze lane also, but nothing else. She was afraid to move along the top of the maze hedge in case some of the shrubs couldn't carry her weight and she fell through. It wouldn't do to break her arm again. Or the other. Or her neck. There was no fixing a broken neck. Not even for a fae with their curative powers.

"Hello!" she called out.

The running footfalls and children's merry laughter instantly died.

But they weren't moving away from where she was. They weren't moving any closer either.

"Hello! Where are you?" she asked in her sweetest voice, aimed at disarming the children.

She thought she heard the nearly silent retreat as the children backed away as quietly as they could. Then when they thought they were far enough away, they took off running.

She let out her breath and tried to get comfortable on the prickly maze top. She imagined the children would quickly tell an adult, the adult would come to see if the children had lied, and then find her, and then hurry off to get someone to bring a ladder and the king.

But no one came. She frowned. Why didn't anyone do as she expected them to do? She lay down on top of the hedge maze, tired of trying to think or plan or do anything, closed her eyes, and fell asleep.

KING TIERNAN WAS tired from the long journey home and trying to eat a meal he didn't want to eat. All he cared about was what had become of his princess. Lord Srenton had not returned, and it had been at least an hour. A young scullery maid, who shouldn't have come into the great hall during the feasting, caught his eye.

Wringing her hands, shifting from one foot to the other, she looked horribly distraught and though he should have let one of his people see to her, he couldn't help himself. She was standing half in the doorway to the great hall and half out, trying to avoid being seen, but her gaze met his, and he was certain she had to have some news of the princess.

"We have not finished the meal. Remain seated and I will return shortly," King Tiernan told his assembled court. If he was making a mistake as far as he thought concerning the maid, he didn't want his whole court knowing of it.

She quickly hid outside the hall as the king stalked out of it and met her. She was teary eyed, and he feared the worst.

"What has happened?"

"Please," she beseeched him, "do not punish my lads, my lord. They mean right and—"

"Jenine, what has happened?" he asked again, pulling her away from the great hall.

"They were running through the hedge maze. They know they're not allowed. But they heard a woman cry out. And they knew the place was haunted, to pay them back for doing what they ought not."

"Where?" he asked, moving her to the inner bailey.

"I would not know, my lord. I've never been inside. 'Tis forbidden for servants."

"Where are your boys?"

"You will not punish..." She hesitated. "I'll fetch them, my lord."

He figured she didn't want to be punished also should she be in trouble for not sending her lads to him. In short order, she had both in hand, dragging them by the arms and handing them off. "Please...," she pleaded one more time.

Tiernan said to the boys, "Show me the place where you heard the lady yelling."

"She's a ghost," the one boy said, his eyes wide, his face as white as the fluffy clouds drifting overhead. "She was calling out in such a sweet voice we knew she meant to eat us. For going into the forbidden maze."

Tiernan glanced at the other boy to see his take on the matter. The other boy bobbed his head up and down, his face just as pale, his eyes just as saucer sized.

"Show me where she is, and I'll let you play in the hedge maze while the courtiers take their meals."

Both boys shook their heads, fear evident in their pale faces.

He'd tried to be nice, but he had to know that if it was the princess, she had not been injured. He took hold of both boys' arms and said, "Show me or you'll both be spending the night in the dungeon, and it is for sure haunted."

At that, the boys both, albeit reluctantly, led the way.

Tiernan had never been in the hedge maze before and if he'd had to discover the location of a missing person, let alone even find his way out, he would have had a time of it, without the use of fae travel.

But after a good twenty minutes when they drew near the place where the boys said they'd heard the voice, he called out, and no one answered. "Princess Ritasia," he shouted again.

Then he looked at the boys. "The maze is bewildering. Are you sure this is where you heard the lady?"

"Aye," they both said.

Tiernan feared the princess had become lost in the hedge maze and was searching for the exit without success. If he moved one way, she could be moving another. He would have to get her knights. He assumed they were dark fae trackers and could at least follow her faery dust trail.

Before they left, one boy called out, "Are ye a ghost, me lady?"

Tiernan waited to hear a reply.

The other boy seemed to gather his courage and shouted, "The king is here with us, and so he said it was all right if we play in the hedge maze!"

No answer.

And then Tiernan swore he heard a faint rustling in the shrubs a short distance off.

Both boys visibly gulped and looked as though they were ready to run away.

"Hello?" a feminine voice said, sounding sleepy, disoriented.

Sweet goddess it was the princess. "Ritasia, where are you?"

He stalked toward the sound of her voice.

"Do not be angry with me," she said.

Angry? He was relieved no harm had come to her. He hurried to where she was, but he saw no sign of her. "Ritasia?"

"Here!"

He frowned. Gods' wounds, she was on the other side of the hedge maze. He glanced back to speak to the boys and have them guide him out of here and to whatever path would take him on the other side of the hedge, but the boys had vanished like will o' wisps, a blink of light, and then gone.

"Damnation!" Now what could he do? He had no idea how to reach her or even how to leave the maze to get help.

"Ritasia, as soon as I can get help, we'll find you and get you out of here."

"No, Tiernan, please do not leave me."

Her voice sounded so pleading, his heart went out to her.

He heard more rustling, and he swore she was trying to claw her way through the hedge maze, but that would have been impossible without a good set of hedge trimmers.

Then he looked up and saw her peering over the edge at him, her dark eyes wide, half of her long hair hung loose from the jeweled combs that had kept them in place, while she was way up on top of the hedge maze, and his heart nearly stopped.

10

Ritasia couldn't have been happier to see anyone in her life than she was to see a very concerned King Tiernan, no longer angry in the least.

"Jump to me," he called out, wearing a very smug smile.

"What? Fairies do not fly!"

"I'll catch you. Hurry, Ritasia. I do not know how long it will take before I can find my own way out and come back for you. I may not remember how to return here. Jump and I'll catch you."

She was sure she looked her usual obstinate self when she was of a different mind than him. "Fine," she finally said. "If I kill you or if this kills me, it will be on your head."

His smile broadened and she thought he had the loveliest smile of any man she'd ever known—part smug, superior male, part relieved to see her being herself.

"About the ring and medallion..."

"We will take care of it together," he agreed.

She would have to remember to shake him up more whenever he thought to dictate to her. It made him much more agreeable.

But his saying so about the jewelry earned her smile, and then she frowned. "Catch me, and do not drop me."

"I am the king, my lady. A hawk fae king does not drop a lady in need of rescuing."

"Yeah, well, remember that when I fall from this height."

With a deep breath, she jumped, hoping she didn't kill the man who still might be her husband. She wasn't sure about that prospect though, even if he was certain she would be his bride.

He caught her as her breath whooshed out in surprise, and she was at once relieved to be down from the top of the hedge and even more so that the king was the only one who knew of her having been up there.

"Light as a feather," he said, smiling down at her, hugging her tight.

She gave a ladylike snort. "You do not have to lie to me. Thank you for coming for me. But you know, if the hedge maze wasn't warded against fae travel, I would have been able to get myself down."

Shaking his head, King Tiernan began to carry her through the maze.

"You can put me down now. I can walk."

"Nay, I prefer it this way."

She got the distinct impression he felt he'd lost her and now he had her under his thumb again, but really in more of a loving way. "I thought you said you didn't know the way out of the maze."

"I haven't a clue. We will walk until we get somewhere, or until someone else comes to rescue us."

"I would have thought you would have played in the maze when you were a boy and knew all the paths," she said. "If it had been me, I would have."

He looked at her, studying her, then nodded. "I can see that you would have. I did not live here as a boy," he said, and his voice sounded rather melancholy.

She looked up at him. "Why not? Did you live in another castle?"

"Aye, I did."

"Oh, then your father wasn't king at first?" she guessed.

"He was king." He let out his breath. "There is much you need to know about the history of our people and how I will be different. First, my father and his father and for generations back, were known as tyrant kings."

"Oh." She'd overheard Duke Tully speaking to Tiernan and saying such a thing but hadn't known if it was the truth or just myth.

"But I am not."

She smiled. Sometimes he was.

He looked down at her and frowned. "Not always. At least I try not to be."

"All right. What else?"

"The son was always exiled."

"Truly? Why?" She couldn't imagine her mother doing that to Deveron when he was born.

"Because the son always killed his father to gain the crown."

She stared at Tiernan in disbelief. He had recently come into power. That's what her brother had said.

"I did not kill my father. I wasn't living in the castle. I only moved in once my father had died, and I was needed to rule."

She didn't say anything for a while. She thought she heard the splashing of water beyond one of the hedges and looked that way but couldn't see anything but greenery and more greenery.

"I did not kill him, Ritasia. I never even really knew him. And I was happy to manage the castle where I lived and fight wars with the island kingdom."

"The island kingdom?"

"Aye, off our western shores."

"All right. What else?"

He didn't speak for some time, and she knew he was deliberating on how to put the next news to her, and she assumed it would not be good.

"My people believe that if the wife of the hawk fae king has more than one child, that child could eventually cause a civil war, fighting the rightful sibling for the throne."

She couldn't help the anxiety she felt now. "If...if your wife had a second child, they would put the child to death?"

He didn't say anything for the longest time, and her skin chilled with fresh concern. "Put me down...my lord."

He wouldn't. Softly, he said, "In the past, an assassin would kill the queen to ensure the king had no more children by her."

"Someone murdered your mother?" she choked out. She couldn't believe any fae kind could be so barbaric. Not of the seelie courts. Unseelie, yes.

"I would not let any harm come to you, Ritasia, believe me."

She didn't think it would be very long before the boys told someone the king was fighting with a ghost in the hedge maze, but when no one came for them, and the king seemed hopelessly lost, he backtracked to where a small hidden garden sat. Inside, water poured out of a sea serpent's mouth into a large copper fountain. That was the delightful sound she'd heard earlier behind the hedge maze.

A wrought iron gazebo sat nearby with a covered roof and a bench for two was situated on the raised wooden floor. He carried her up the steps to the gazebo.

But now she wanted to leave this kingdom far behind. She cared for Tiernan. Truly she did. But she wasn't about to give him a child, then worry some assassin would murder her to keep the royal house in order. And she wouldn't allow a child of hers to be exiled, but if she didn't live beyond its birth, she really wouldn't have any say in the child's upbringing anyway.

"Put...me...down!"

He did this time, setting her on the bench in the gazebo, then crouched before her and took her hands in his, his touch tender. "I swear to you, Ritasia, I will keep you safe. I have already rewritten the laws concerning the banishment of any children I have, and that if I have a hundred, it will not be enough."

She pulled her hands free and folded her arms across her chest. "Speak for yourself, your lordship."

He smiled, took her hand in his, and kissed it. "I have further decreed that if anyone should attempt to murder my queen, the assassin and his entire family will die."

She frowned. "The assassin, certainly, but his family?"

"If he frets about his family, he will not risk the attempt on your life. In the past, it was the way of doing business, and any assassin felt obligated to do the job."

"By the king's orders?" Ritasia asked, aghast.

"I do not know for certain. All I can do is state what I will and will not allow while I rule."

"Is that the reason you came in search of a bride far from your home?" she asked. "I saw the way the women of your court wouldn't meet your eyes. How they seemed afraid of getting to know me."

"I want to change the rules of the kingdom. If it meant finding you in another kingdom far away, the effort was worth it. This place," he said, motioning toward the grounds, "would not be a home. Not without you here to share it with me. It has never been my home."

"Can you show me where you lived as a boy?"

"Aye. Tomorrow. But today, I must get you out of the hedge maze and have someone make a map of it for me if I ever venture here with you again."

"Nay, the adventure is discovering the paths ourselves."

He seemed pleased she would say so. Something they would do together in the future.

"But what of the ring and medallion?"

"We'll get rid of the power as soon as we're discovered. As to Romero..."

"I'm sorry about what I said concerning him, given the circumstances of him being here."

"Aye, but what I wished you to know is that he is a good fellow, has been loyal to me since I was exiled, and though he appears to be a young man, he is not. He also was gifted, which is why a fae brought him to live among us in the first place."

"Gifted? In what way?"

"He can read minds. No one, but the fae who brought him here and I, knows of this. Not even my advisor. Romero keeps his gift a secret for good reason, but he liked me, despite my being a tyrant prince..."

Ritasia smiled.

Tiernan gave her a quick smile in return and continued, "Mayhap because he was exiled with me at my birth. He was shunned as a human, once the fae who brought him here died. And so he shared with me his secret so that I could use his services. He is a means by which I can know the truth in people's thoughts. He will inform us if anyone is even thinking of harming you."

"But he cannot read all minds at once, can he?"

"Nay. But he will monitor thoughts as he serves you."

She considered Tiernan's sincerity. He had been truthful when he could have hidden all that concerned her until she was wed to him and then? It would have been too late.

"You will be my bride, you know."

"You have so many beautiful women in your court who would be at your beck and call," she reminded him, throwing his words back at him from the earlier conversation they'd had at her castle during the meal.

He smiled. "In tears and fearful. Not like you."

Ritasia choked on a laugh. "Whereas with me, you get this." She motioned to the gardens.

"Aye, and the exploration of dangerous, ancient ruins. And trips to the unseelie plane of existence."

"You really don't mind?"

His voice and expression darkened. "It seems I don't have much of a choice."

She raised her brows.

"I'm hopelessly in love with you." He shrugged as if it was an affliction he couldn't overcome.

"I will stay a month," she said, "or less if I feel I cannot live by your rules."

"I challenge you to make your home here with us...with me and help me to change the way my people view its rulers." And with that declaration, he bent his head and for the second time, he pressed his mouth against hers, lightly at first, a whisper of a kiss, seeking her participation. She kissed him back this time, surer of herself than last time, surer of him, feeling a smile against her mouth, knowing she had pleased him.

"Not a month," he mouthed against her lips, the heat spiraling through her veins. "I couldn't live that long without saying the vows."

She nudged his lips and kissed him again and he obliged, pulling her against him closer, deepening the kiss as if she'd already agreed to the marriage plans.

When she and he were like this together, she felt the world would cease to exist, and she would be happy as long as she was with him.

Then they heard voices calling out their names. Her knights. And several others conversing behind them as they led the pack, following her fairy dust trail. She and Tiernan were hidden in the gardens still, but he didn't pull away from her as if wanting to prove to everyone he'd claimed her, and she'd claimed him right back.

"Princess Ritasia!" Sir Conklin called.

"Here!" she said.

Lord Srenton yelled, "They're in the secret garden. Wait here." Then he slipped into the garden through the barely visible entrance, as if afraid of what he might find.

"Did you locate Romero?" King Tiernan asked, as he led Ritasia out of the gazebo, his hand grasping hers.

"He went fishing, my lord."

Tiernan frowned. "Fishing?"

Lord Srenton shrugged. "He likes to fish at the river, Cook told me. I found him there, but he hadn't seen any sign of the princess. Then I came across Jenine's lads, and they said you were fighting a ghost in the hedge maze. The princess's knights located your trails and here we are."

His advisor looked at Ritasia and then again at the king, his silent question—would the princess wed the king?

The king glanced down at Ritasia, noticed how disheveled she looked from catching her hair on the prickly shrubs and pulling it loose from the combs, how wrinkled her gown was from the flight, and figured no matter how innocent his handling of the princess had been, no one would believe their story.

Lord Srenton looked hopeful that now they would wed, though knew not to ask.

Once they had returned to the keep, his courtiers silently watching him and his princess bride—as soon as she agreed—King Tiernan leaned down to kiss her cheek, holding her hand firmly in his, trying to show that they were fine together.

Ritasia blushed. He loved it when the color rose high in her cheeks. And then she gave him a look as though she knew just why he had kissed her.

His people still waited, watching to see if she would shun him, to see if she felt for him what had to be evident that he felt for her. She blushed again. "Ritasia," he whispered to her and wrapped his arm around her waist, pulling her snug.

He wanted her to show that she cared about him like he knew she did when they didn't have an audience. But she remained stiff, and he motioned with his free hand to Sophia, saw Romero, and said, "Come with the princess and me. We need to discuss something important."

Lord Srenton cleared his throat.

Tiernan glanced back at him. "You as well, of course."

And then they stalked to his solar where he would get this business with the ring done and over with.

In his private chamber, sunlight streamed through a large window, the black leather chairs trimmed in brass, seeming to absorb some of the light, while dark tapestries covering the walls grabbed more of it. In one corner sat his dark wooden desk, and along one wall a row of bookcases. None of this was his, truly. His world was at the castle where he'd been raised. This was his father's solar and so was everything in this castle.

He noted how depressing the atmosphere was in the room and decided then he would have to make some changes. "Mayhap after we take care of this other matter," Tiernan said to Ritasia, "you can help me to decide how to lighten up the mood in this room."

"It is the king's solar," Sophia said, her words brittle.

He had never seen his mage look so waspish before, her brows pinched in a tight frown, her mouth curved down, making her look as though she'd swallowed something that had spoiled.

"Aye, it is," Tiernan said, pointedly. "And a place where I shall go with my queen to read or whatever else we might have in mind to do."

He noted Romero's smile and wished then the human couldn't read all his thoughts. "Therefore, I wish the place redecorated so that it pleases her."

His advisor looked pleased with his comments, and so did Romero as he leaned his back against one of the walls, arms folded across his chest, looking like a teen, but with the eyes of an ancient human.

"If I should stay," Ritasia carefully said, giving Tiernan her full attention, "I would be happy to do so."

"What is it you wished of me?" Sophia snapped, not hiding her animosity. Not even using his title.

"King Tiernan," Ritasia reminded her, "or...my lord. Do you think as a mage you do not have to be courteous to your betters?"

The gold ring around the mage's eyes glowed. "Betters? Just because you were born to a queen doesn't make you better than me."

Tiernan didn't believe Ritasia felt that way either, but he could see that she wasn't going to take any guff from the mage. And he could see her point. The woman *had* overstepped her bounds.

"Princess Ritasia is correct. It seems my title has been lost to you, Sophia. Be sure to use it when appropriate from now on."

That got him a look of shocked hurt from the mage, and then she turned her glower on the princess. "King Tiernan," she said, still glowering at Ritasia.

"Aye, we have a matter that a mage must deal with," the king said.

"Why is *she* here?" Sophia asked, glowering at Ritasia, sounding surly and maybe a little *jealous*? "I do not perform my miracles for all to see."

Before Ritasia could take her to task, whether or not she was some powerful hawk fae mage and might be able to turn her into a toad, Tiernan said with harsh criticism, "These are Princess Ritasia's artifacts, not mine. She is the keeper of them until we render them useless." Though he did not owe her an explanation. Had he been a tyrant, he would have told her to do what he wished and that would have been that.

Sophia turned her scowl on Romero next, although Ritasia knew the woman wasn't satisfied with the king's answer. "And him? I do not entertain the masses. Especially not humans."

"Sophia," Tiernan said in evident exasperation. "If you wish, I will call on Eleron. *He* can take care of this matter."

Ritasia was beginning to believe the mage was a spoiled diva. Most likely always getting her way because of her special talents. But Ritasia didn't care for the hateful glances the woman cast her way.

But then Sophia smiled, and the look was purely predatory.

Feeling uneasy about the mage's demands, Ritasia squeezed Tiernan's arm. "Eleron will do." As if Ritasia had any say in the matter, and she had no idea who this other mage was or how powerful either.

She wasn't certain Sophia should even touch the objects, let alone attempt to dispel the magic in them.

Ritasia was certain only the ring held the power. The medallion was just the symbol of the unseelie. But why Minova would have taken it, Ritasia couldn't figure. If the woman thought to hide what she was, she couldn't have.

Unless...if she could create such a powerfully magic item, maybe the queen could disguise her seelie scent and the fact that she had gold rather than silver rings around her eyes. Then if she wore the medallion of the Na, they would think she truly was one of their royal members.

Rethinking that scenario, Ritasia frowned. The queen would be recognized as not living amongst the Na, no matter what magical tricks she used. Unless...well, maybe she could control minds and suggest she was one of them.

Maybe.

Tiernan first handed the medallion over to Sophia. The mage examined it carefully, her face brightening with dark interest. "Unseelie," she said, then turned to the king. "From the kingdom of Na. Where did you get this?"

"As I said, it is the princess's."

She glanced at Ritasia, looked as though she hated to have to ask her, but said in a barely controlled, annoyed voice, "Where, Princess Ritasia?"

"Why from Queen Minova." Ritasia said it as if any fool would know it and that didn't everyone receive such a gift from the ancient queen?

"It's unseelie. She was...she was the queen who stole magic from the unseelie court of Na."

"You know of her?" Ritasia asked, surprised.

"Doesn't everyone?" Then the mage gave her a simpering look. "Well, mayhap only mages because she was thought to be one of the most powerful mages alive." She darted a look at the king. "What else do you have?"

"Is the medallion empowered with magic?" he asked.

She shook her head, her eyes focused on his hand where he held the ring in his fist. "What is the other item?"

"A ring." He opened his palm and held the silver band up for her to see.

She stared at it, then looked up at him. "It looks so plain."

That's what Ritasia had thought. The only ring in the queen's jewelry box that wasn't covered in gems. No thief would think to steal it because it looked so commonly plain.

As if the object was something delectable to eat, Sophia licked her lips and stared at the ring. "What is the problem with it? You wished me to do something with it?"

"Is it magical?" he asked.

"I would have to hold it to feel if it has any power," she said.

"You cannot tell from just looking at it?" Ritasia asked, her voice rife with disbelief. "I thought a powerful mage could see the magic emanating from the object."

Sophia snorted. "Shows what you know about magic."

And then everything happened so quickly, Ritasia and everyone else was stunned momentarily into inaction.

The mage grabbed the ring from Tiernan's outstretched palm and slipped it onto her finger. The king seized her wrist.

Romero shouted, "No!"

And Sophia and the king vanished.

Lord Srenton cursed aloud, then said, "Stay here, princess. I'll get the guards and your knights." Then he hurried out of the room.

Ritasia's thoughts swirled as she tried to think of what to do. If the mage hadn't taken Tiernan to the unseelie plane, anywhere she took him in the human world, if that's where she had gone, could catch the unseelie's attention.

Romero quickly said, "Take me with you."

She turned and stared at him.

"I serve you. I serve him. I pledged my loyalty to him when he was but a lad because he had been kind to me when others had not. And you, because he asked me to. But when you wanted me returned to the human world—"

"I'm so sorry..."

"No, don't be. I saw in you a heart of gold."

"But we cannot follow him. Not without the ring."

He took her hand and turned it so that her palm was down. "What do you see there?"

She stared at the band of silver engraved with the Celtic symbol on her finger once again. "I...I don't understand."

"The ring called to you when you were in Queen Minova's chamber."

"How do you—"

"I read your mind, princess. Sophia thinks she has the ring and medallion, but it is the ring that has the power. She saw it, just as you had suspected. The ring has a blue aura. It appears that only a descendent of the queen can wear the ring and make it work."

"She's..." Ritasia looked from Romero to the ring, trying to make sense of it all. She shifted her gaze to the human. "The dark fae descended from her people?"

"A good probability. Sophia will most likely go to the human plane. But she won't be able to reach the unseelie one. Not unless *you* take her there."

"Where is she?" Ritasia asked, glancing around at the floor. She was a dark fae tracker, but before she could follow after the mage and the king, Romero grabbed her arm.

Then he bowed his head. "Take me with you. You cannot go alone."

"Aye, of course." She took his hand. "I hope this doesn't make you ill."

"Like it does you?"

She frowned. "I don't want the world to know."

"'Tis our secret."

Then with murder in her heart, she followed the red trail left by Sophia and the silver one left by the king through the black void of space, watching the sparkles twinkle like tiny bits of glitter barely visible to the naked fae eye.

When they appeared in a town, Romero said, "This is Edinburgh."

"Scotland?" she asked, surprised.

"Aye. Where did they go?"

She looked down at the sidewalk and began tracking the king and Sophia's trail. "This way." She stopped, then looked at a pub situated at the corner of two streets, Celtic music drifting from the gray stone building, that appeared to be as ancient as her own castle. "They're in there."

"I'm sorry, princess," Romero said, his expression full of true remorse. "I did not see what the mage planned until she considered it and then it was too late for me to warn you and the king."

"It's all right," she said, seething, heading for the door to the pub. "Too bad you couldn't know what was in a person's heart before they thought about it."

He said very seriously, "I know what's in your heart. You believe you are a dark fae, but you are one of us."

She thought about how he had called himself one of the hawk fae when he was but a human and so many seemed to scorn him.

Apparently reading her thoughts, he said, "I have been with the hawk fae for longer than I was with my own kind. I may not have the fae ability to travel, but my father, the fae who brought me here, gave me semi-immortality the same as the fae have, the same healing properties—"

"The same need to fit in," she softly said. "Do not think to serve me."

He raised his brows in question.

She stopped at the door and took his hands. "Be my friend instead." And for a brief instant she thought of the human girl Cassie and how she didn't want her to be hurt by the fae.

He bowed his head over their clasped hands reverently. "Always and forever, my princess, who shall be queen."

She snorted. "The king has sent you to work on me, to wear me down until I say I will wed him."

Romero stifled a smile. "He could do much worse."

She couldn't help but like Romero.

When they walked inside, the bar was crowded with men sitting on high stools at the counter, their feet resting on brass footrests, conversation and laughter loud over the music playing overhead. Men and woman sat drinking at small tables throughout the establishment. The pub was dark and smoky.

"I do not see them," Romero said.

"This way." She took his hand and led him through the noisy place, but before they reached the kitchen, she saw the trail had shimmered a little way into the area and faded. Disappointment and concern washed over her. "They're not here any longer. I bet that she is trying to find a way into the unseelie realm."

"WHAT THE HELL do you think you're doing, Sophia?" Tiernan asked, jerking her wrist toward him so he could remove the Celtic ring from her finger.

"Why didn't you take interest in me?" Sophia sniped. "I could have been anything you wanted. Why did you have to bring that dark fae here to our kingdom? She doesn't belong here."

"What do you want with the ring?"

"I've heard of the magic in the kingdom of Na. Of Queen Minova and her traipsing between planes, of stealing magical knowledge for her own. Until they caught her. But I'll be cleverer than she was. I won't get caught. Send the dark fae princess back home. I'll be your queen. And I'll do anything you ask of me."

"Destroy the power of the ring then."

She gave him such a sinister smile, he grabbed for the hilt of his sword.

"I can make the metal melt in your hand," she said.

"Hand over the ring."

She admired it and smiled at him again. "This is my home. Now that you are the king and have changed the rules about how long your queen shall live, I would have to take on that role."

"You had nothing to do with my father's death, had you?"

"Why ever would I have done something to him?"

"He didn't require another queen."

She shrugged. "You should be pleased that you now reign in his place."

He calculated whether he could cut her down before she could cast a spell and assumed he could not. But he was certain now that she had something to do with his father's death.

He tried to reason with her. "If you go to the unseelie plane, they will not welcome you."

She raised her brows. "Why, Tiernan, I'm a powerful mage."

He lunged for her and as soon as he seized her wrist, she transported him to another place. But it was still the human plane of existence. She cursed.

He nearly smiled, glad she hadn't managed to move them to the unseelie world, but he was certain if any unseelie managed to follow them here from Na, they would recognize him at once.

~

RITASIA TRANSPORTED Romero and herself again until they reached another town, mist rising from a lake and all the buildings were made of gray stone, rolling emerald-green hills set as a backdrop above the homes. It was beautiful and if she'd had a moment to cherish the beauty, she would have.

The fairy dust trail led them to another pub, the men seated inside while the women were sitting outside drinking while watching their kids.

Then she saw the king and Sophia. He was furious with his mage, red-faced and giving her a tongue-lashing. She looked just as angry. Probably because she couldn't make the ring do what she wanted it to do.

"Are you looking for this?" Ritasia asked, raising her hand and showing off the ring.

Sophia stared at her as if stupefied, glanced at her own ring and saw it vanish right off her finger.

Queen Minova must have made a ring that created the illusion that another could wear it, but it would not take the bearer to the unseelie plane. Why had it remained with the king all that time and not reappeared on Ritasia's finger? Most likely because he had not intended to use the ring and had not placed it on his own finger.

"Ritasia!" the king shouted, heading for her just as she heard movement behind her.

12

Ritasia turned and saw at least a half dozen male unseelie headed straight for her, one shouting, "Grab her!"

All were running toward her, and her heart couldn't pump any faster as she struggled to remove the ring. Before she could slip it off and return to the safety of Tiernan's castle, Tiernan seized her arm, but so did one of the unseelie fae. She knew she and the king were doomed as soon as she fae traveled and found herself in the middle of an unseelie gathering in a large great hall in some drafty castle.

All unseelie gazes shot to them. The seelie in their midst. But she still worried about Romero and the wicked mage they'd left behind.

"We come in peace," Ritasia quickly said, as guards hurried to surround them. "I swear that we intended to destroy the...this ability to come here, but your people stopped us."

"Lies," several said as the tension like the electricity from the slow buildup of a thunderstorm charged the air.

"Queen Minova, an ancient seelie fae, discovered a way to breech the unseelie plane," Ritasia continued, trying to sound brave. Actually, she was still so angry with Sophia that she thought she sounded more like a pissed-off fae that was ready to eat unseelie for dessert.

Tiernan was standing very close to her, his hand on the hilt of his sword, but he couldn't fight all these fae. She, likewise, was ready to pull out her dagger.

"Queen Minova and her people are at the fae kingdom of Na," an older unseelie fae said, his beard long and white, his fingers stroking the fine hair. He reminded her of one of her dark fae scholars.

"Aye. Well, I mean, that's what my mother assumed from ancient documents left in Queen Minova's ruins."

The man surveyed her through cold gray eyes and cocked his head. "You do not look like the queen."

"Aye, she does," another interjected, stalking into the room. This man was a few years older than Ritasia, the silver rings around his gray eyes glowing brightly. "Strip her. Find the device she used to break through the fabric separating our worlds, then kill her." He glanced over at Tiernan. "And kill him. First."

"No!" She screamed, grabbed Tiernan's arm and without having the time to think of where to go, she transported them to the same pub in Scotland. Seeing the place, she was relieved to have escaped the unseelie, but they had to return to King Tiernan's castle to really be safe.

Sophia was gone. But Romero had no way to fae transport without the help of a fae.

"King Tiernan, princess!" he shouted and hurried to join them.

The king was busy trying to get the ring off Ritasia's finger.

But the unseelie fae arrived first.

Ritasia jerked out her dagger, but this time two of the unseelie had fae irons and before Tiernan could withdraw his sword, manacles were placed on both the king's and Ritasia's ankles. And then the unseelie whisked them away. Back to the unseelie court and their fate.

Her heart pounding with fear and frustration, Ritasia was quickly disarmed as the guards ripped the dagger from her fingers, and then she was roughly hauled to a private chamber, though she did not go without a fight.

She managed to knee one of the men in the place her brother had taught her, bringing the guard to his knees. He couldn't even do much more than cry and groan. She was grateful for her brother's teaching.

But then a fist smacked her in the temple and her head spun out of control. She was jerked off her feet, and the guard threw her over his shoulder. Her kicks and hits to his body earned her a slew of curses from him.

One of his companions laughed. "She is not what we envisioned, eh? A dark fae wildcat! Remove her claws and teeth and she will not be so unmanageable."

The one carrying her grunted. "Tell that to Han, who she has nearly unmanned with her knee."

He stalked into a chamber all dressed in burgundy from the cloaked bed to the tapestries hanging on the walls and covering the floors. One of the women following them yanked open the curtains to the bed. The guard threw Ritasia on the down-filled mattress. The room smelled like jasmine, and she assumed it was a woman's chamber.

"Strip out of your clothes. If you do not do so willingly, I will be back to help." He stalked out of the chamber with three other male guards and slammed the door.

She couldn't understand why they wouldn't have just removed her ring, figuring it would have been the source of her power to move between planes, but it had disappeared. Had it slipped off in the struggle she'd had with the men?

Women entered the room in a hurry and hovered over her.

"Take off your clothes," one of the older ones warned.

Wanting to fight them, she knew it would only get the guards' attention, and she didn't want their filthy hands on her. She quickly obliged, knowing they would find nothing to explain her abilities.

They searched her clothes as the older woman watched, her violet eyes hard, her lips stretched taut in a fixed line. "Why are you here?"

"I explained. I wish to get rid of whatever is causing me to visit the unseelie world. I do not wish anyone harm."

The woman lifted a brow skeptically. "You have come for someone?"

Ritasia shook her head. "I was shocked the first time I ended up in the unseelie world. I didn't know how it had happened, nor did I know how to return to my world."

"Where is the ring?" the woman asked.

One of the women handed Ritasia's gown back to her. Another offered her shift, while another, her boots, and stockings.

The woman must have seen the ring on Ritasia's finger before she lost it. Ritasia didn't say anything, instead just quickly redressed herself.

"Search the corridor and great hall. She believes it slipped off her finger before she arrived in the chamber."

The woman could read her thoughts?

The woman's unsmiling mouth curved up just a hint.

Like Romero, Ritasia thought.

"Who is Romero?" the woman asked.

"A human servant in King Tiernan's employ."

"Does she speak the truth?" a younger woman asked, whose face was harder, her expression more calculating. She kept clenching and unclenching her fists.

"Aye. She speaks the truth." She turned to the younger woman. "Call the guards. Have the areas searched for the ring. Tell that wisp of a Na woman that she can see this one for just a moment in the dungeon where she will be locked."

Na woman? Not the redheaded witch.

Ritasia's thoughts earned her a true smile from the woman's lips.

The others watched the woman's expression change and the younger one said, "What has she revealed?"

"That Listra is a witch."

All the women smiled at that. But then the guards returned and the one did as before, threw her over his shoulder, not waiting for her reaction.

"Let me down, you barbarian! I can walk!"

But he didn't listen to her as she saw the women searching the corridor for any sign of the ring. She hoped they would never find it. That it had slipped into a crevice and was gone forever.

Then to her astonishment, she was taken into the dark recesses of a dungeon and locked in a cell with King Tiernan. On her feet again, she rushed forth to embrace him, though he was already on his way to intercept her.

"Tiernan," she said through tears, but his mouth was already on hers, his hands running up and down her arms as if making sure she truly was real and alive and well.

His sword and dirk had been removed, but seeing the bruises discoloring his face, she assumed they had not had an easy time of it when taking the weapons from him. But at least they had not killed him. She wondered what had changed their minds. Maybe the loss of the ring.

"Are you all right, Ritasia?" he asked, gathering her in his arms and then carried her to a narrow wooden bed, not unlike the one at Ritasia's castle dungeon.

"The ring," she whispered. "I lost it."

He glanced down at her finger. "It must have slipped off when you struggled with the guards." He shook his head and moved her to the bed where they sat down next to each other.

"I worry about Romero."

"Romero? As soon as one of your knights locates our trail, they'll give him a ride home. It is us that you need worry about."

"I'm so sorry I got us into this in the first place."

"If you had not, someone else might have."

"But possibly only my mother could compel the ring to do her bidding. Or my brother." Tiernan didn't say anything and Ritasia stroked his arms in a loving, conciliatory caress. "I'm so sorry. I would do anything to make this up to you, if I could."

"Marry me." He looked so sincere, his forceful gaze almost commanding her to agree.

She frowned up at him. "You cannot be serious. Our very lives are at stake."

"Aye."

She shook her head.

"I challenge you to marry me," he insisted, kissing her forehead.

She deepened her frown. "You've said that before. Challenged me. Why?"

"Prince Raglan said that you never back down from one of your brother's challenges."

She gave a short, disbelieving laugh. "It never entailed marrying someone."

He brushed strands of hair away from her face. "Marry me, Ritasia. And no matter what happens, you will have made me the happiest king alive."

"I feel terrible about this," she said, motioning to the cell and their predicament. She rested her head against his chest, listened to the thunderous beat of his heart, wanting more than anything to be able to transport them out of their predicament. How much longer would they have together?

She believed those in charge here were meeting to decide their fates. She doubted the outcome concerning them would be favorable. Unless they couldn't find the ring. And then they might just keep them here forever, locked away.

"So make it right," Tiernan said, brushing his mouth against her throat, making her relax just a bit, warming her in the chilly, damp cell.

"Making it right means I could get us out of here," she whispered, feeling boneless in his embrace.

"You will. Just say you wish to marry me."

She took a deep breath and meant what she said next. "Tiernan, with all my heart I would marry you, but..."

He put his finger to her lips. "No buts. No regrets. Just marry me."

She realized then she truly did want to, but she didn't know his people yet. Then again, she would have years to garner their friendship. And though she wanted to be well loved by his people, it would take time, if only she and Tiernan were given the chance to make it work.

Footfalls clomped along the stone floor headed in their direction, and Ritasia stiffened. Tiernan was immediately on his feet, standing in front of Ritasia, protecting her.

"This is highly irregular, my lady. If the king hears of it, it would be my head," the guard said.

"The queen said I may see the prisoners," she said, and Ritasia recognized the voice. The red-haired unseelie witch from South Padre Island. What was she doing here?

Ritasia stood and took Tiernan's hand. He looked down at her, his eyes filled with admiration and love.

They were in this together. She would not allow him to be her protector. They would do all they could to protect each other. And pray it was enough.

"All right, here they are," the guard said, giving the unseelie a look of annoyance, and then he turned his scowl on Ritasia and Tiernan.

The woman looked through the bars at Ritasia and frowned. Her red hair was piled up on top of her head, and she was wearing a black gown with a low-cut bodice, but she still was a lot more clothed than the time when Ritasia had seen her at South Padre Island in the skimpy bikini.

Then the woman turned to the guard. "Go."

"But..."

"Go!"

He shuffled off, cursing and muttering under his breath.

"So," the unseelie said to Ritasia, her eyes bright with recrimination, arms folded across her chest, "what brings you here?"

"I wondered the same of you," Ritasia said. "You are of the kingdom of Na, are you not? Why are you so far from home?"

"I want the ring," the woman said, not bandying words about it any further. "I want it now."

Ritasia looked at her finger, knowing the ring was not there, and yet it was, as if it had been invisible all this time. She took a startled breath. "It won't work for you."

The unseelie's eyes narrowed. "How do you know?"

"Are you a descendent of Queen Minova?"

The unseelie turned her head slightly to consider Ritasia's words, then gave her a brief smile, but her look was dark and calculating. "Give me the ring, and I will have you released."

"You don't have the power." Ritasia guessed the rulers here would not allow an unseelie outsider release them.

The woman ground her teeth. "Who says you should have the ring and not me? She is my many-times-removed great aunt."

Ritasia's mouth dropped open. "Who are you?"

"Listra, and you are Ritasia."

"But you're unseelie."

"Aye."

"She, the queen—that is—is seelie."

"True enough."

But now Ritasia wondered if the woman was really a descendent of the queen—though how could she be when she was unseelie—if the ring would work for her. She wanted to test the theory, to offer her the ring, and see if it would work. But what if it did? Then she and the king would be stuck here until the unseelie disposed of them.

"You are saying Queen Minova had a lover who was unseelie?"

Listra looked at her as if the thought nauseated her, but then she nodded. "Aye."

"And she had children by this union?"

"Six, three girls and three boys."

"But...did they live?"

"Of course. What do you think? We eat our own kind?"

"They would have been half my kind."

"Aye, and half mine," Listra said, sounding annoyed.

"Who was her lover?"

"No one of importance. Give me the ring." Listra reached her hand through the bars, palm up.

Tiernan was staring at the unseelie, so he still didn't know about the ring when Ritasia said to Listra, "If you will free us from here and allow us to return to the human world, I will give you the ring, and we'll go back to our seelie plane."

Tiernan studied Ritasia, the questioning in his gaze asking her what she was doing. She placed her hand over his fingers that still held her other hand, and that's when he saw the ring.

Listra glanced back down the corridor, then looked again at Ritasia and the king. "You will try to trick me. You'll go straight to the seelie plane, and I will have lost this opportunity to have the ring."

"What do you want it for?"

Listra shrugged. "What anyone might want. Power."

"You cannot give it to her," Tiernan said, shaking his head emphatically. "The ring is entrusted to your care."

"To free us from here, I will do anything."

"I will free the king, then come back for you," Listra said slyly, her hands gripping the bars of the cell.

"No, the both of us at the same time. You could lock him away somewhere else in the unseelie kingdom, and I wouldn't know until it was too late."

"Distrusting, aren't we? All right. Wait here."

As soon as the unseelie stalked off, Tiernan said, "I don't trust her."

"I don't see that we have much of a choice."

Before they could say anything more to each other, the spiteful fae was back, carrying a ring of keys.

Ritasia wondered what Listra had done to the guard.

The unseelie unlocked the door to the cell, then joined them. "Okay," the woman said, hurrying to unlock their manacles, her hands shaking so badly, King Tiernan took the ring of keys from her and finished the job.

Listra seized Ritasia's arm. The king held Ritasia's free hand, and they returned to the pub where they'd been previously. Poor Romero was talking to a couple of fae, explaining King Tiernan's plight and the plight of his bride, but when he saw the king and Ritasia, he rushed to greet them.

"Give me the ring," the unseelie said, her hand outstretched, palm up.

Ritasia did as she requested. A deal was a deal even if made under coercion with one of the unseelie, like making a deal with the devil, she thought.

Ritasia grabbed Romero's and the king's hands and transported them to the gardens outside his castle before they could again be incarcerated in the unseelie kingdom.

"I didn't want to go inside the castle," she said, "in case we ran into Sophia. You must get hold of your other mage and have him stop her."

"The ring," Tiernan said, still holding Ritasia's hand.

Romero stuck his own hands in his pockets and moved a couple of paces away to give them a bit of privacy.

Tiernan tenderly touched Ritasia's face. "You shouldn't have given it to her."

"I had promised." She sighed, then glanced at her hand where the ring had been, but now her finger was bare. She looked up at the king. "Now Listra will be the only one they're after."

Tiernan didn't look pleased, but he nodded, then he turned to Romero. "Discretely, find Eleron. We need his help right away."

Romero bowed, then slipped out of the gardens.

"She's a mage," Ritasia warned.

"And I'm a battle-trained king," Tiernan said and at that moment he looked like one hot-headed tyrant of a king, ready to take on the world.

Something crashed on an upper floor and screams resounded.

"Stay here," Tiernan ordered Ritasia.

He tore out of the gardens, but Ritasia couldn't wait here. She ran after him, trying to keep up with his long stride as he raced into the keep.

But as she entered through the doorway, she saw him running up the stairs to the upper floors and smelled smoke.

"Fire!" someone shouted.

There was so much noise and commotion on the upper floors and smoke drifting down the stairs from the floor above that she didn't see Sophia was headed straight for her until it was nearly too late.

"You have Queen Minova's ability to deceive, I see," Sophia said coldly. "But she was only a mage by magical artifacts. I, on the other hand, come by it naturally."

"So you believe that makes you, Sophia, the mighty mage more...powerful?" Ritasia hoped her words would carry and someone would hear her.

The woman smiled. "Oh, aye. That I am. Give me the ring, and no tricks now."

"I don't have it," Ritasia said, matter-of-factly. "I bargained for the king and my freedom and gave it to an unseelie fae."

"You would *not* have done such a thing. No seelie in their right mind would have given such power to an unseelie." Then she twisted her head a little as if she was reconsidering her words. "Or you lie. Either you have it, or the king does. Which means I have to kill you first as it seems the ring has taken a liking to you. Finders keepers, mayhap. Once I find it, then it will owe allegiance to me. And *only* me."

"Why would you want to go to the unseelie court?" Ritasia asked, not understanding the draw when undoubtedly, they would want her death if she went there.

"They have magic we know little about," she said. "You, of all people, should know that. That's why Minova went there in the first place."

"She had a lover."

Sophia scowled. "No."

"Aye, and six children by him."

"No!" Sophia raised her hand, and Ritasia knew that the mage planned to conjure up magic that would destroy her.

She raised her own hands in defense as if that would stop the woman, who was crazed with the lust for power.

Ritasia briefly saw the ring on her finger, just as the mage did.

"You lied to me!" Sophia screamed. "I knew it!"

Before Ritasia could get over her surprise at the sudden appearance of the ring, streaks of white-hot light shot from the mage's fingertips and sailed across the room directed at Ritasia. Before it reached her, the beam of light bounced back without even touching her as if an invisible wall separated the two women. The energy that Sophia had cast at Ritasia returned in full force and struck the startled mage in the chest. The jolt of power threw her against the wall. She screamed and sank to the floor.

Clutching her chest, Sophia grimaced in pain and rolled onto her side, unable to get to her feet.

"You will die for that, Minova!" Sophia screamed.

The queen? "You knew Minova?"

Sophia growled, "We were sisters, did you not really know? Only she would not share her power with me."

"Sisters? So you *did* know her. But not just because she was a mage. If you had the natural mage abilities, why would you need her magical artifacts?"

Sophia's eyes were gold ringed daggers, but she wouldn't reply. Ritasia knew why. Sophia hadn't been as powerful as her sister. She wanted to be just like her or even more powerful.

"Did you know she had a lover?" Ritasia asked, figuring she had to have known.

Sophia snapped, "The Na prince. His father was ready to kill them both! But when she was with child, he couldn't do it."

Ritasia stared at her in astonishment. "She loved an unseelie *prince*?" So the unseelie had lied to her also. She had said Minova's lover had been no one of consequence.

"Aye. Minova was crazy. I told her so. Our people followed her and ended up with her in a court of their own, prisoners forever." Sophia seemed lost in some distant memory, her eyes shimmering with tears as she stared at the ceiling.

And for the first time, Ritasia saw a woman who was hurting, both emotionally and physically.

"You wanted to see her? To use the ring to see her?" Ritasia could imagine how horrible it would be if she'd lost her brother in such a way, never getting to see him again. She would want to rescue him as soon as fae possible.

Sophia clucked. "I...wanted...to...destroy...her. And...that... useless prince. As they destroyed everything I loved."

"She was in love."

"Ha! And the king was tired of his son moping about her and so he took her prisoner as soon as he was able. Forced her to stay there so she could no longer return to the seelie world."

"But you're so young."

"Fae glamor, dear." Sophia coughed up blood and spat it out.

"But...if you're her sister, why didn't the ring work for you? Or for the unseelie who claimed Queen Minova was her great aunt, many times removed?"

Sophia cleared the blood from the corners of her mouth with a swipe of her arm, the ring around her eyes still glowing hot gold. "Apparently, the ring chose you. But now I believe if you were dead, I would have a chance to wield its power."

Ritasia didn't believe the mage would ever be able to call upon the ring's power. "How did you end up here? In King Tiernan's court?"

"The castle suffered a major earthquake. I thought those of us who were left would all die. The keep collapsed in ruins. Those of us who survived moved on. Here, I was a mage, but no one knew of my connection to the woman who could have caused a rift between the unseelie and seelie planes. She should have been despised, hated for what she had done. Instead, everyone loved her," Sophia spit out. "The unseelie, our people. I was no longer a princess. No longer the queen for the short time I took power after our own queen deserted us for an unseelie prince."

So that's why the woman felt she didn't need to acknowledge King Tiernan's title as king, not when she had become queen in her own right. But then her people had abandoned her for her sister. How that must have wounded her.

"Why did you not look for the ring in the queen's chambers?"

"She had taken it with her. Or so I had thought." Sophia smiled bitterly. "Where did you find it?"

"In her jewelry chest among her other rings."

Sophia shook her head, looking defeated. "I would never have thought the ring that yielded such power would be so plain."

Which Ritasia was certain was the reason Minova had crafted it as such. But Ritasia still couldn't understand her own connection to Queen Minova. "How could the dark fae be descendants of the queen if her children were unseelie?"

"Your people are *not* descendants of the queen's unseelie offspring," Sophia said angrily. "But a daughter she had before Minova got mixed up with the unseelie prince. The daughter had run away. Some say she lived with the sphinx fae, the oldest fae civilization still in existence, and that her offspring eventually moved to the area where the dark fae now rule. As to my sister, you are *nothing* but her servant." Sophia raised one hand.

"No!" three ladies screamed, and Ritasia glanced briefly to see some of Tiernan's courtiers watching what was going on.

Ritasia, fearing the mage would attempt to kill her, again held up her hands as if she could deflect or redirect the woman's spell.

A red laser light flashed across the room toward Ritasia, but then twirled around and headed straight for the mage. It struck her in the heart, and she screamed. "How? How are you doing that?" Her words were raspy and harsh.

Ritasia *was* deflecting her spells. Not creating the weapon of destruction but redirecting the killing force back on its creator. If Minova was so evil that she had wanted more power by stealing from the unseelie, why did she create a ring—as that must be what was channeling the energy—as a defensive rather than an offensive weapon?

She didn't think Minova had any evil intentions.

Sophia's face was gray, her eyes half shut. She barely raised her hand off the floor and sent a shimmer of blue light that dribbled across the stone floor and petered out. Her eyes grew dull and lifeless, and she lay very still. Ritasia thought she was dead, but she didn't draw closer in case she wasn't.

"She killed her," one of the women sobbed.

But Ritasia couldn't quit staring at the mage who had wished to kill her, still fearful the woman would come to life and try again.

"My lady," a woman said, but she was standing so very far away, and she didn't draw any closer.

"Tell the king!" another said, who sounded as though she was standing near the other woman.

"Get the king at once," a man said. "My lady..."

Several people rushed down the stairs, though she couldn't look to see who was coming. She couldn't tear her gaze away from Sophia. The mage had been Queen Minova's own sister. And in a very distant way, Sophia had been related to Ritasia and her dark fae brethren.

Smoke snaked down the staircase, and she could hear people shouting and coughing. Out of the confusion, several ran down to the first floor where she stood frozen.

Footfalls ran toward her. And before she could see him, Tiernan dragged her into his arms. He looked shocked to see her in the keep when he'd told her to stay in the gardens. But then he saw Sophia, gray and wizened, lying on the floor on the other side of the room, her glamor that would have made her appear youthful still, gone.

Ritasia hadn't realized she'd been trembling or that tears were running down in rivulets against her cheeks until she leaned against his strength, and he kissed away her tears.

A physician quickly checked the mage's heart. "She is dead, my king."

Tiernan said, "Have her taken away and cremated. Have Eleron ensure her ashes hold no magical power."

To a still stunned Ritasia at the turn of events, Tiernan said, "You will marry me."

It wasn't a question or an offer. But a command.

"She wasn't evil," Ritasia said, kissing Tiernan back, finally breaking free of the shock as two men quickly removed the mage's body from the great hall.

"Aye, she was. She would have killed you."

"Sophia, aye. Well, mayhap not even her. She had lost everything. Her home, her family, her people, her position. Minova was in love with an unseelie prince. She...she saved my life."

Tiernan studied her as she frowned up at him, then he slid his hands over the ring on her finger and raised a brow. "I'm glad. You will be my wife. No one will think to threaten your life, not after you eliminated the most powerful hawk fae mage in our kingdom."

"But we have to destroy the ring."

"I'm beginning to believe there was a reason for you finding it."

"To protect me?"

"Aye."

"But what about fae travel? And what about the unseelie?"

"If you remove the ring before you fae travel, you do not arrive at an unseelie court."

"But I'll never be able to travel to the human plane either."

"Perhaps you can learn how to use the ring to protect yourself from the unseelie when you visit the human world. Or mayhap my remaining mage can remove the ring's ability to take you to the unseelie world. We'll figure out a way to solve the problem one way or another. Now about our marriage..."

"Not before I have any say in it," Queen Irenis said, stalking into the castle with Deveron, his bride-to-be, Alicia, and Ritasia's cousins Niall and even Micala in tow.

Ritasia's mouth parted, but she couldn't say anything. Her family must have taken a flight shortly after they did. But why had they come? Not that she wasn't glad to see them, but she just couldn't believe it.

"My lady," Tiernan said graciously greeting her with a low bow. He didn't look concerned that her mother might try to prevent the marriage.

"When our men searched Queen Minova's chambers, they found her journal," Queen Irenis said, "which is the reason why we have come unannounced."

Romero said, "She was in love with an unseelie prince."

The queen frowned at him, and he instantly looked chagrined, and held his tongue.

Ritasia knew the page must have read her mother's mind and in his exuberance to tell all, he'd spoken when he shouldn't have. Her mother wished to tell the tale and would not suffer someone to beat her to it.

The queen then turned to Ritasia and added, "She met him in the human world, fell in love, and found a way to imbue the ring with power that would allow her to slip into the unseelie world and see him."

"She was in love with him," Ritasia whispered, squeezing Tiernan's hand. "She wasn't trying to steal magical secrets from the unseelie world."

"You're correct, Ritasia," her mother said. "His father discovered their secret rendezvous and when she was in the human world, he had his men take her prisoner. But he did not do it to keep them apart. His son was hiding the fact that he had fallen in love with a seelie queen and was disconsolate about every betrothal his father tried to get him to agree to.

"When the king learned who was responsible, he decided Minova would join the unseelie court one way or another. He was not allowing his son to live in the seelie kingdom, but if she refused, he intended to eliminate her as an obstacle to his son's future happiness. Until he discovered she was with child, which was the grandchild of the unseelie king. Minova made the ultimate sacrifice —giving up her kingdom and the love of her people, to be with the prince she loved."

"But he was unseelie," Ritasia said, still not able to fathom it.

"Aye. Her people were so melancholy at losing their queen that the unseelie king took pity on them and gathered those up that he could when they looked for her in the human world and brought them to his court so that they could continue to attend their seelie queen."

"But how did anyone know that's what happened?"

"The king allowed one of the women to be returned who had left a husband behind. She wrote what had happened and left the journal in the queen's chamber for anyone to find later who wished to know what had become of the queen and her people. An earthquake later destroyed the castle and everyone else moved away."

"Including the woman and her husband?"

"Aye, I suppose."

"But then why would the unseelie want to kill me? Or King Tiernan when we arrived at the unseelie court?"

"I suspect that the word had spread that you intended to give the queen whatever device she had used to travel between the planes and free her. She is forever tied to the unseelie court. She might look like us, but she has become one of them."

"Then we must destroy the ring."

"Keep it. Use it for your protection. If we can find a way to dispel the ring's ability to take you to the unseelie realm, we'll do it. Now, about another matter. Do you wish to marry this king, or should we take you home? Deveron swears no one can protect you like he can."

Ritasia smiled at her brother.

"I dare you to prove me otherwise," Deveron said, a wicked gleam in his eye.

Ritasia stiffened. This was one challenge she didn't need. "King Tiernan said that marrying me at the end of the month…"

"Would be too long in coming," Tiernan said. "Your family is here. Let the proceedings begin."

No one moved an inch. Not his people. Not hers. As if waiting for her agreement.

Tiernan frowned. Then roared, "Now!"

That's what everyone expected of him. Their tyrant king with his thunderous voice proclaiming everyone was to do as he wished. His people hurried to put everything in place.

Except Ritasia knew what the king was really like under that gruff posturing.

And someday, she knew his people would realize it too. But it might take some years.

HOURS LATER, they all gathered in the great hall in their finery, and not only did they celebrate the wedding between the dark fae princess and the hawk fae king, but she said a prayer of well wishes to the seelie queen and her beloved unseelie prince.

This time at the feast, Ritasia ate heartily as the musicians played, even stealing olives and bites of cheese from the king's plate, to his dark amusement, and Deveron shared his food with his betrothed, Princess Alicia.

Tiernan couldn't have been more pleased to have found the princess of his dreams, an adventurous vixen sure to give him gray hairs way before his time. But he would love every minute of being with her—no matter the circumstances.

She smiled up at him, his bride, his wife, his hawk fae queen, and he wondered just what kind of trouble she would be into next. But he cherished her for being just who she was. Free-spirited, kind-hearted, willing to risk her own life for others, and though she hadn't always looked or acted the part—his queen, who was perfect for him in *every* way.

ABOUT THE AUTHOR

USA Today bestselling and award-winning author **Terry Spear** has written over ninety paranormal romance novels, young adult, and medieval Highland historical romances. Her first werewolf romance, *Heart of the Wolf,* was named a 2008 *Publishers Weekly*'s Best Book of the Year, and her subsequent titles have garnered high praise and hit the *USA Today* bestseller list. A retired officer of the U.S. Army Reserves, Terry lives in Spring, Texas, where she is working on her next werewolf romance, shapeshifting jaguars, cougar shifters, vampires, hot Highlanders, and having fun with her young adult novels, helping with her granddaughter and grandson and raising two havanese. For more information, please visit www.terryspear.com, or follow her on Twitter, @TerrySpear.

She is also on Facebook at https://www.facebook.com/Terry-SpearParanormalRomantics.

And on Wordpress at: Terry Spear's Shifters http://terryspear.-wordpress.com/

And her Wilde & Woolley Bears, award-winning teddy bears, that have found homes all over the world: www.celticbears.com

DRAGON FAE

The World of Fae, Book 5

Terry Spear

∽

The Dragon Fae
Copyright © 2012 by Terry Spear

Discover more about Terry Spear at:
http://www.terryspear.com/

To Caryn Block, who was not a YA reader, but who fell in love with the fae world I created, thanks so much! And thanks to readers for loving the series, like Debra Rodriguez, asking me to make Alicia and Deveron's dream come true!

P rincess Alicia of the dragon fae hated having to break Cassie's heart and knew it would destroy their friendship, but she had to take drastic measures if her best friend was to be saved from her own folly.

Alicia was still furious with Deveron, the crown prince of the dark fae. He should have made his cousin, Micala, stay away from her human friend. She feared that Micala would attempt to use fairy magic on Cassie and take her to the fae world, and then she would be a human stuck there. It wasn't right. Cassie would never fully be accepted as one of the fae.

Forced to attend mandatory meetings, schooling, and parties, due to her social status as the princess of the dragon fae, Alicia had not been able to leave Crislis Castle located in the heart of the Morcalon territory, until today. She had two days' break before she had to return to her studies.

She fully intended to take this matter with Cassie into her own hands, although she was supposed to sneak off to see Deveron as soon as her studies were done. The fault was all his that she would have to take drastic measures such as these and save her friend instead. Maybe he would learn how important this was to her if she cut her time with him short.

Before anybody could stop her—because even though she had a break from her schooling, it didn't mean she could avoid other social obligations that could pop up at any time—she willed herself to fae travel to the high school where Cassie was attending one of her classes.

As soon as Alicia transported to the high school, she felt her stomach revolt. She hated this part of fae travel and didn't think she'd ever get over feeling in this way. Hand clutching her waist and swallowing involuntarily to keep the bile down, she tried to will the nausea away. At least she was invisible to the humans so no one could see her bent over in pain.

She had appeared in one of the school's hallways—empty while everyone was in class. The English classes were held down this hall. She remembered them well when she had gone to school here. She had not wanted to ever return to the high school and would have preferred seeing Cassie after class, but her own schedule, and worry she'd get sidetracked if she hadn't left the castle at once, meant she didn't have the luxury to go there as she pleased.

Alicia wasn't enrolled in the school any longer, not since she'd had to "move" away. Who knew that meant to become a princess in a faraway land?

She had no idea which class Cassie was in at this time of day, having given up on trying to keep up with Cassie's schedule when Alicia could barely find the time to visit her except on school breaks when she wasn't seeing Deveron. Which meant she saw Cassie when she was being more closely supervised because she wasn't *supposed* to be spending time with Deveron at all, by order of the king, her grandfather.

She hurried into the girls' restroom, so that she could appear in her human form there without anyone seeing her, and caught sight of herself in one of the big mirrors. She stared at her fae clothes.

Great. She'd been in such a rush, she was still dressed in a forest green hunting gown she loved to wear when practicing her archery skills. The dark green velvet was perfect for the chillier outdoor temperatures, perfect for blending into the woods, and perfect for moving about freely—in a fae world. In the human's? She looked like she was being cast as a princess in a *Snow White and the Seven Dwarves* movie. Except she was blond and not a raven-haired beauty. Her eyes were blue though. All she needed were the seven dwarves. The handsome prince, Deveron, was currently on her list. Not in a good way.

So she didn't need him on this venture either. He would have said he'd take care of the situation with Micala, *again*. And nothing would have come of it. She'd learned that though Deveron was a dark fae and had a dark temper to match, he also had a good-hearted side. She believed that's why he couldn't force Micala to do his bidding where Cassie was concerned. That meant Alicia had to take charge of the problem and tackle this from the human's side of the equation. Which since she'd been one, only she knew how to do.

She considered her gown again, so used to wearing them in the fae world they were second nature to her now. When she first started wearing them, she kept feeling like she was dressing up for Halloween, and she had desperately wanted her jeans and T-shirts and sneakers back. She was allowed to wear them only when she visited the human's world. *By order of the king.* Others in the dragon fae kingdom could get away with what they wished to wear. Not her.

She could have returned to her bedchamber, risked getting stopped, or...suck it up and look for Cassie, ignoring all the kids' stares and comments.

Her blond hair was bound in curls on top of her head held in place by emerald decorated gold pins. She considered letting her hair down and tucking the pins into the leather pouch hanging on the gold belt slung low on her waist. She'd look a little more... normal.

She snorted. If she was going to play the part of a princess, she'd go as she was. She stalked off in her brown suede knee-high boots. The skirt was split up the sides for easy movement, which was one of the reasons she really loved this dress. She looked like she was wearing an outfit that Renaissance fairgoers would pay a hefty price for—*if* she was at a Renaissance fair.

As soon as she walked into the hall, the bell buzzed for the end of the period. Students poured out of doorways like an army of ants rushing to the next meal, except they were confused and going in all different directions. Every eye that caught sight of her, lingered on her hair, her dress, her boots.

She heard comments of "Omigod." "For real?" "Drama class is

on the other side of the school." "Freak." "Love your dress." And so forth.

Then she saw a couple of girls she recognized. Not friends. Just former classmates.

"Hey," Lisa, the blonde, said, "Cassie said you moved away. I didn't realize it was to some fantasy land."

Alicia gave her a wry smile. She would keep her cool, thinking that if they had spoken to Cassie, maybe they knew where she was now. "Do you know where Cassie is going next period?"

The other girl, Dana, shook her head, her red gold curls tossing about her shoulders. "But we're getting together for lunch at the chicken wings place across the street if you want to join us the period after next."

"Thanks, I will." This time she gave them a grateful smile. They looked like they were up to something. She knew that look. Like Deveron would give his sister when he was about to play a joke on her. Or like when his sister gave him the same evil look.

What to do in the meantime. What she'd love to do was just... vanish. Give the girls something to think about if they thought to pull anything mean on her.

She headed for the school office. Maybe she could still locate Cassie before the lunch period.

She tried to ignore all the comments about her dress, about being out of place, about being a weirdo, or gorgeous, the wolf whistles from a couple of guys, and tons of flat-out stares. What caught her attention were three cool-looking guys that appeared like they could be playing on the football team, cute, but not interested in her like she was date-material. All had on jeans and sneakers, one wearing a T-shirt with a Celtic cross, one with a skull, and the other, just a plain navy blue shirt—no fashion statement at all.

They reminded her of a pack of wolves as they tensed, muscles bunching, a feral look crossing their facial features. The warning couldn't be ignored. They were human so she didn't know what the trouble was, though she'd been afraid at first they might have been some of the unseelie. She'd learned from Deveron's sister, Ritasia, how she'd run into some and the trouble she'd had. But these guys weren't fae. They would have had a shimmering aura around their human form, and when angered, rings around their eyes would glow—gold for seelie, silver for unseelie.

Yet they considered her with a condemning look that made her skin prickle with unease.

She tilted her chin up, challenging them to do anything that she would take as aggression on their part. But they stayed where they were, watching her, as if letting her know she couldn't get away with anything while they had her in their sights.

She slipped into the school office and closed the door behind her. A secretary sat at a desk, two students waiting for parents to bring them proper clothes as one boy's seat of his pants hung down past the crack in his butt and his sweatshirt barely reached past his naval. The girl wore a shirt that was way too see-through, the semi-sheer white fabric clearly showing off a black lace bra.

The secretary looked up from her computer and stared at Alicia's costume. It was busty, but it was supposed to be for the... uhm, period look. If the woman decided Alicia had to stay and wait for her mother to come bring her a change of clothes, she'd be in real trouble. First, Alicia didn't attend the school. Second, her mother was back at the dragon fae castle, wearing a retaining collar, courtesy of Alicia's grandfather, who wouldn't let her mother leave the castle grounds. And third, there was no way to get hold of anyone else who could bring her a change of clothes, unless they were of the fae. Making a phone call to them? Wouldn't work.

"Nice costume," the lady said.

Alicia took a steadying breath and smiled. "Thank you. I need to get hold of Cassie Wimberley. We were supposed to get together because her mom's taking me home with them after school, but I can't remember where she is next period."

The secretary looked down at the monitor, typed in Cassie's name, and said, "English lit. But you'll be late for your own class. She's in Mrs. Jenkins's class, room 134."

"I'll meet her at the end of class period. Thank you," Alicia said brightly and hurried out of the office before the secretary asked her anything that she couldn't answer honestly.

She had no intention of waiting until lunch time to see if she could meet up with Cassie. What if the two girls who had told her about the chicken wing place had set her up?

She didn't want to just walk into class and explain she was a new student or anything either, certain Cassie would be so excited, she'd be upset with her when Alicia told her it wasn't true. So she'd go as a fae, invisible to everyone.

Walking into the nearest girls' restroom, she found three girls redoing their lipstick or washing their hands, and Alicia ducked into a stall.

The girls laughed, and she assumed it had to do with her *costume*. She didn't hear them leave the bathroom, but she wasn't waiting around for them to exit the room. She walked through the bathroom door, invisible to the girls who were whispering to each other and staring at the stall Alicia had been in. She desperately wanted to walk up to them and speak, maybe ask them what they were whispering about. And see *their* reaction.

She sighed. If she had been raised by the fae, she probably would have. The fae were known to be tricksters, playing games on the humans, doing anything in their power to take advantage of the humans for their own amusement. Since she had been raised as a human, she didn't like the notion at all. She wondered then if someone's environment did greatly influence the person. Or if her personality was such, she just wasn't into playing tricks on others.

She walked past them and through the door to the hall. It was clear now, and she hurried back to the English class where Cassie would be taking studious notes. Finding the right class, Alicia walked through the door and saw Cassie sitting on the far side of the room... taking studious notes. She smiled. She liked it when some things in life were always predictable.

Cassie's gorgeous fall of brown hair curled about her shoulders, her dark brown eyes reading the whiteboard where the teacher was busy scribbling notes.

Some of the students were reading books other than their text-books. One was doodling on a piece of paper in his notebook. Another was sleeping. Or at least he had his eyes closed and appeared to be sleeping.

One of the boys she'd seen standing with the other two in the hall who had been watching her as she went to the school office—one of the ones she'd thought of as a wolf who was wearing the shirt with the skull—was now observing her, his blue eyes wide with shock.

Her mouth gaped. *Oh...my...God.* He could see her. *As the fae.* Just like the time she saw Deveron's friends as the fae that they were. And just like she knew Deveron was one of them. The dark fae. Dangerous to anyone who was a fae seer.

She froze in place, having intended to take an empty seat on this side of the classroom where there was a vacant seat near the door.

He quickly looked away, his blond locks hiding his expression. So he wasn't such a wolf after all. Not when he knew she knew he could see her. When no one in the room should have been able to.

And not now that he didn't have his wolf mates to back him up.

He was texting, warning his friends that the fae had come after him, she suspected. In her fae history books, she had read about a number of cases where the fae had killed people like him because they could see them. She couldn't imagine anything so horrible. The humans who were fae seers couldn't do anything to the fae. So why did her people need to eliminate them?

Yet a cold shiver ran up her spine with the notion that he could not only *see* her but knew just what she was when no one should have known. *No one human.* She realized that she was feeling as though she was something alien, something that needed to be eliminated in their world.

Why could he see her? Was he partly fae? And the other two boys? Were they also?

This was *so* not good.

She decided to do what she knew she shouldn't, what she *wouldn't* do at any other time, but she *was* the fae. She might as well get used to the idea.

Heading for the boy with the phone, who was *not* supposed to be texting in the class anyway, she walked straight through the kids and their desks.

She'd barely reached him when he caught sight of her standing beside him, just before she yanked the phone out of his hand.

He gasped, nearly fell from his seat, staring up at her, his eyes darkening and widening at the same time as if he was looking into the eyes of a ghost. Or something worse. A fae who could kill him.

Trying for sweet and innocent and friendly, she smiled down at him and mouthed the words, "Thank you."

He still stared back at her with wide-eyed shock. With his phone clutched tightly in her hand, she turned and headed straight through the kids, the closest shot to the door, holding the phone above their heads. The tricky part was that she had no idea what to do about his phone. It was visible when she was not. The only way to make it invisible was for her to appear human, and then return to her invisible state to make the object in her hand invisible also. She couldn't appear human in class suddenly, or she might cause a wild panic.

Instead, the cell floated over the kids' heads. Most were too wrapped up in reading their books or other activities that were keeping them occupied that they didn't see the phone. A couple of girls' mouths gaped as they watched the phone float toward the door. She couldn't help that.

When Alicia reached the door, she realized she couldn't take the phone through the door like this. She opened the door, walked out of the class with the phone in hand, and closed the door.

And screamed as hands quickly encircled her wrists with iron manacles.

~

NOTE TO READERS:

DON'T you love when there's a cliff hanger, AND the next book is already available? Have fun reading Dragon Fae! Terry Spear

ALSO BY TERRY SPEAR

Adult Titles

Romantic Suspense: Deadly Fortunes, In the Dead of the Night, Relative Danger, Bound by Danger

***

The Highlanders Series: His Wild Highland Lass (novella), Vexing the Highlander (novella), Winning the Highlander's Heart, The Accidental Highland Hero, Highland Rake, Taming the Wild Highlander, The Highlander, Her Highland Hero, The Viking's Highland Lass, My Highlander

Other historical romances: Lady Caroline & the Egotistical Earl, A Ghost of a Chance at Love

***

Heart of the Wolf Series: Heart of the Wolf, Destiny of the Wolf, To Tempt the Wolf, Legend of the White Wolf, Seduced by the Wolf, Wolf Fever, Heart of the Highland Wolf, Dreaming of the Wolf, A SEAL in Wolf's Clothing, A Howl for a Highlander, A Highland Werewolf Wedding, A SEAL Wolf Christmas, Silence of the Wolf, Hero of a Highland Wolf, A Highland Wolf Christmas; SEAL Wolf Hunting; A Silver Wolf Christmas, SEAL Wolf in Too Deep, Alpha Wolf Need Not Apply, Between a Wolf and a Hard Place, SEAL Wolf Undercover, Dreaming of a White Wolf Christmas, Flight of the White Wolf, All's Fair in Love and Wolf, A Billionaire Wolf for Christmas, SEAL Wolf Surrender, Silver Town Wolf: Home for the Holidays, Night of the Billionaire Wolf, You Had Me at Wolf, Joy to the Wolves, The Wolf Wore Plaid, Jingle Bell Wolf, The Best of Both Wolves, While the Wolf's Away, Christmas Wolf Surprise, Wolf Takes the

Lead, Wolf on the Wild Side, Her Wolf for the Holidays, A Good Wolf is Hard to Find (2024), Dreaming of a Highland Wolf (2024), Mated for Christmas (2024)

SEAL Wolves: To Tempt the Wolf, A SEAL in Wolf's Clothing, A SEAL Wolf Christmas; SEAL Wolf Hunting, A SEAL Wolf in Too Deep, SEAL Wolf Undercover, SEAL Wolf Surrender

Silver Town Wolves: Destiny of the Wolf, Wolf Fever, Dreaming of the Wolf, Silence of the Wolf; A Silver Wolf Christmas, Between a Wolf and a Hard Place, Home for the Holidays, Jingle Bell Wolf

Wolff Family Lodge Wolves: You Had Me at Wolf, Wolf on the Wild Side, A Good Wolf is Hard to Find

Highland Wolves: Heart of the Highland Wolf, A Howl for a Highlander, A Highland Werewolf Wedding, Hero of a Highland Wolf, A Highland Wolf Christmas, The Wolf Wore Plaid, Her Wolf for the Holidays, Dreaming of a Highland Wolf

Billionaire Wolf Series: A Billionaire in Wolf's Clothing, A Billionaire Wolf for Christmas, Night of the Billionaire Wolf, Wolf Takes the Lead

White Wolf Series: Legend of the White Wolf, Dreaming of a White Wolf Christmas, Flight of the White Wolf, While the Wolf's Away, Mated for Christmas

Red Wolf Series: Seduced by the Wolf, Joy to the Wolves, The Best of Both Wolves, Christmas Wolf Surprise

Wolf Novellas: Day of the Wolf, Seal Wolf Pursuit, Wolf to the Rescue, Night of the Wolf, United Shifter Force

***

Heart of the Jaguar Series: Savage Hunger, Jaguar Fever, Jaguar Hunt, Jaguar Pride, A Very Jaguar Christmas, You Had Me at Jaguar, The Witch and the Jaguar, Dawn of the Jaguar

***

Heart of the Cougar Series: Cougar's Mate, Call of the Cougar, Taming the Wild Cougar, Covert Cougar Christmas, a novella, Double Cougar Trouble, Cougar Undercover, Cougar Magic, Cougar Halloween Mischief, Falling for the Cougar, Cougar Christmas Calamity, Catch the Cougar (Halloween Novella), You Had Me at Cougar, Saving the White Cougar, Big Cat Magic

***

White Bear Series: Loving the White Bear, Claiming the White Bear, Bear of a Halloween

Grizzly Bear Series: Bear in Mind

***

Wolves of Old: Wolf Pack

Vampire romances: Killing the Bloodlust, Deadly Liaisons, Huntress for Hire, Forbidden Love, Deadly Liaisons, Vampire Redemption, Primal Desire, Huntress Unleashed

Vampire Novellas: The Siren's Lure, Vampiric Calling, Seducing the Huntress

***

Comedy Romance: Exchanging Grooms, Marriage, Las Vegas Style

***

Science Fiction: Galaxy Warrior

Young Adult Titles

The World of Fae:

The Dark Fae

The Deadly Fae

The Winged Fae

The Ancient Fae

Dragon Fae

Hawk Fae

Phantom Fae

Golden Fae

Falcon Fae

Woodland Fae

Angel Fae

***

The World of Elf:

The Shadow Elf

The Darkland Elf

Warrior Elf

***

Blood Moon Series:

Kiss of the Vampire

Bite of the Vampire

Night of the Vampire

The Vampire Chronicles Series:

The Vampire in My Dreams

Demon Guardian Series:

The Trouble with Demons

Demon Trouble, Too

Demon Hunter

Non-Series for Now:

Ghostly Liaisons

The Beast Within

Courtly Masquerade

Deidre's Secret

The Magic of Inherian:

The Scepter of Salvation

The Mage of Monrovia

Emerald Isle of Mists